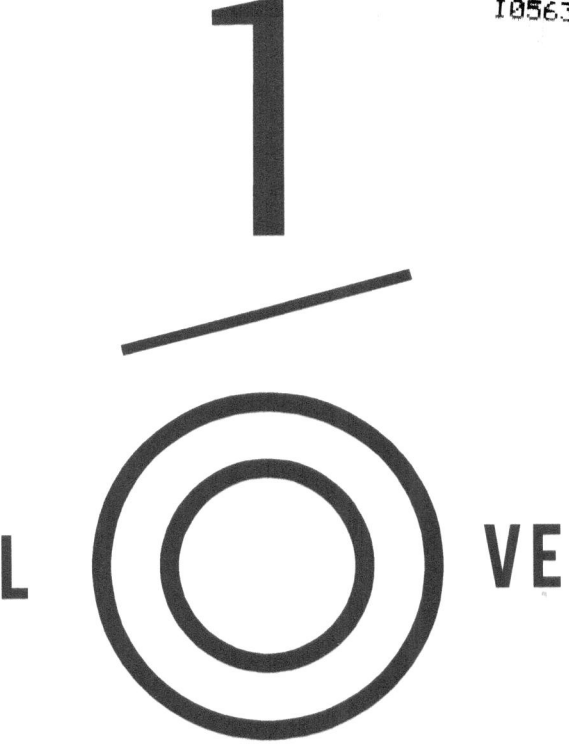

1/LOVE

VISHWAKARMA PUBLICATIONS VP

Prashant Ingole

One Love

First Edition : July 2015
© Prashant Ingole

ISBN 978-93-83572-47-2

Published by:
Vishwakarma Publications
283, Budhwar Peth, Near City Post,
Pune - 411 002.
Phone No: 020 20261157
Email: info@vpindia.co.in
Website: www.vpindia.co.in

Typeset, Layout & Images
Meghnad Deodhar
Vishwakarma Publications.

1 JOB

All I remember when I finished my graduation in 2000 was, there was nothing for me to look forward to, no dreams, no aspirations and nowhere to go. My head was in a mess - a chaos exactly like our parliament, filled with dumb politicians who don't know what to say when it's important. The sheer commotion and confusion inside me had only one solution - a Job.

"Which Job shall I try for?" I asked myself. This disorder has often been with me, talking to myself, when puzzled or thrilled. Still, what kind of question was that? As if I had a wide choice of jobs to choose from. It was at the same level as going to a Vada-Pav stall, and wondering what to order. Any ways, whenever I was confused or nervous, I asked these silly questions to myself, either looking into the mirror or looking at the wall. Whether the wall was painted beautifully or plain wasn't important but staring at it was.

This had been happening for quite some time. It was already July, and my first decision of choosing commerce in college, left me with very few options. It's likely that some of you would have gone through this after finishing school like me. We were so busy enjoying our school life, painting, drawing, cricket, football or doing whatever the guy next door did; we forgot to plan our future. This forced us to take either Arts or Commerce, instead of becoming an engineer or even doing something creative, for that matter. "Future is never calculated in accountancy classes, but analyzed with a foresight for which a classroom is not needed." I read this somewhere. Oh no, I am sorry! I wrote it in my book myself after my college certification. Anyways, here I was holding a degree in my hand from the University of Pune, giving me little scope for employment.

"What is this going to get you?" I said again to myself, looking at the certificate. . I was staring at it, thinking of how I could get a job, as my marks were very minimal, or let me say I just managed to graduate. The highest marks I had ever secured, was 48% in the 10th grade.

I never fared better than that, and it dipped as I graduated. I got 42% in the final year. I was average in everything, my looks, my studies and my dress sense, except at talking to women. I never charmed them with my first look, but yes, once I got a chance to speak to them; they were all mine. I had at least one above-the-average quality!

I always thought, that all commerce graduates work in banks, shops or at those places where stupid calculation comes into play, but I had only 52 marks in accounting, which was the highest among all the subjects, and it was a big achievement for me in hindsight.

I still remember the day, when I saw an advertisement in the newspaper in the evening. I was a bad reader, trust me, I could finish a whole 30 page newspaper in 5 minutes flat, skimming through the pictures and headlines, especially if the pictures were of hot girls or some famous personalities. I called the office where a job had been available to check if they still had the vacancy.

"Hi, this is Nikhil" I spoke in the politest way possible.

"Yes Nikhil! What can I do for you?" said a girl in a sweet tone.

"I read your advertisement in today's newspaper; do you have a vacancy for a fresher?" I asked.

"Yes, we do" she said in an even sweeter tone. In fact, everyone sounds beautiful on the phone, don't they?

I was asked to come for a personal interview. I don't know how it all happened, but I was selected. I was to come to know the reason very soon. It was –the clearing house of ABC bank in Pune. I was happy that I got a job, with a salary of Rs 3,000, which was a very good amount in those days. My job was to handle cheques which came in for clearing in the bank, sounds interesting doesn't it? I always thought of endorsing one big cheque in my favour one day. And that was my dream.

Anyway, I got the job and started going to work. My first day, when I entered the office, well, let me call it a house under clearing. It was an apartment converted into an office. When I entered wearing formals, everyone seemed shocked, because it was a casual atmosphere in there, with people focused only on the work. Abhijeet, my manager introduced me to all the staff members.

"Friends, this is Nikhil Ranade, our new employee. He will be with us from today," said Abhijeet and asked everyone to introduce themselves to me; they did so with a broad smile. They all had one thing in common, the smile, as if they were posing for a wedding photograph. "Hi Nikhil, I am Rakesh," said one of the guys in a husky voice like Shakti Kapoor's and laughed like Prem Chopra.

"Hi," I said to him and shook hands. Everyone still had that smile; honestly speaking, they all looked dumb to me. I believe I was the only one who was holding a bachelor's degree in the volume of 10 employees. That's when I realized the reason for my selection. Other than my Boss and his subordinates, everyone was either a 10th or 12th

Standard pass out. Guess what? Those guys also drew almost the same amount of salary as I did. Shame on me, my smile shrunk as I came to know about this in the afternoon during lunch. Everyone was pleased other than me, as the happiness cheque, which I had been carrying in my heart had just bounced.

Work started. Initially I felt good that at last I had a job. But then days passed by faster than I thought. I was 4 months old in the so-called clearing house system, when I realized that it was a very mechanical Job. Sitting on the computer, tallying the cheques and making entries ... I started getting bored. While making an entry, I looked around and saw everyone busy on their computers looking like robots, programmed for a specific task. All I could hear all day was the keys on their keyboards, and that too was irritating.

One day, I was reaching home, my sweet home, a small row-house in Koregaon Park, where I lived with my mother, father and two younger sisters. Koregaon Park is famous for the Osho Commune, which was just 2 kilometers from my house. A huge terrace, open to the sky, a botanical garden in front of my house, the back of the house looking on to farms - it was truly heaven for us. My father, a retired Colonel from the Indian Army had now turned to a businessman, and managed a security agency post-retirement. He was so busy in his work and business, that he couldn't guide me enough. And whenever he tried to, I would take it in the wrong way, so he gave up. My mom was a housewife, and like every mother, sweet and caring. I had two beautiful young sisters, who were studying in college. The youngest one was in Junior College, studying Arts, and the elder one was pursuing interior designing. I was the eldest. I came home that evening and spoke to my dad. Dad, being an army man and strict in the real sense, one had to be careful, when talking or even thinking about talking to him.

"Dad, I am getting bored at this job," I said.

"Why? What happened?" he asked, and he stopped doing what he was doing. He was busy writing some notes in his book. That is what most of the retired people seem to do; keep a check on the smallest thing and make an entry of everything possible, sneezing as well.

Whenever we both got into conversation, everyone was keen to be there in the drawing room with us, as there was always a chance of some enraged talks between us. We both used to talk on some very basic topics, but the intensity would be as if we were discussing a rock solid conflict like the J&K issue.

"I don't know, but it's a very mechanical job, nothing new to do, the same-old thing every day." I muttered.

"Son, I had already told you to help me in business, but you never heard me. Moreover, you wanted to be the Boss and do what you like," he said and continued calculating something and scribbling in his book.

"Yeah, right, I know who would be the Boss. You would keep me working like a dog tied to a leash in your hand," I thought of saying but kept quiet, nodding.

Before I joined this job, Dad had asked me to join him in his business, which I declined, thinking, managing security guards is as bad as guiding a donkey to cross the road. Besides, I never wanted to argue with him every day.

"But Dad, I wanted to know what a job is like. I would love to join you, but I want to work for some more time to get the experience," I said, pretending that I would join him one day, which I knew was next to impossible.

He looked at me for a moment, keeping his pen aside. "So why are you asking me?" he replied, folding his hands as if praying to me to be quiet.

Meanwhile, my mom entered the drawing room from her own battlefield 'The Kitchen'. She may have sensed the heat building up between us.

"Then why don't you change your job if you are not happy?" she said after taking a seat next to me on the sofa.

I was happy that she agreed with my unspoken idea. Frankly speaking, such kinds of ideas came to me in abundance, and my family was aware of it.

"That's what I am thinking, Mom," I added.

For any mother, the most important things for her are her kids, and their comforts.

My dad said, "Whatever you do in life; you have to plan and do it. You just can't do things randomly."

"That is just what I am good at - doing things RANDOMLY. How can you keep off from doing things which you are so good at?" I was about to say, but my mom nodded significantly, asking me to cool down and not be stupid.

"But Dad, I am looking for a similar job," I went on with sheer excitement, ignoring Mom.

To that he had a great statement as a reply "If you keep options open in life, you are bound to fail. Cut loose all your options and just follow one thing, and then only can you win." He left the room with his register on this note and went to his bedroom.

I still remember those words loud and clear. But I couldn't understand it then, and made fun of him once he left. My mom went back into the kitchen, and I was left behind, with the temperature soaring high in the drawing room, with random thoughts in my mind. The next morning as I got up, I snatched the newspaper from my sisters; they both were busy reading their horoscopes.

"Hey!" they shouted "We are reading can't you see?"

"There are better things to do, than reading the horoscope in the morning," I uttered.

I don't understand, what inspires girls to leave everything aside, and first thing in the morning, read this diluted version of your future. Or let me say, whenever they see newspapers, all they want to see is their horoscopes. God save them.

"Maa, see Nikhu is troubling us; he is not letting us read the paper" they shouted to Mom in unison; she was inside.

Mom shouted in return from inside "Hey Nikhil! Why are you bothering them? Let them read."

I had already taken the paper and started my hunt. "I am looking for jobs, Mom, and they are just reading that stupid Sun sign stuff and bogus things like that" I shouted back.

Mom came out with chapati dough in her hand and told them "You can read your horoscope later, let him see what he wants first" After saying this she went back. They were not happy at all; I started mocking them, making faces.

I went through the papers, flipping the classifieds and then read something called Operations Co-ordinator. That word itself encouraged me to call them up. I was a man on operation, "Operation Job." I was called for an interview.

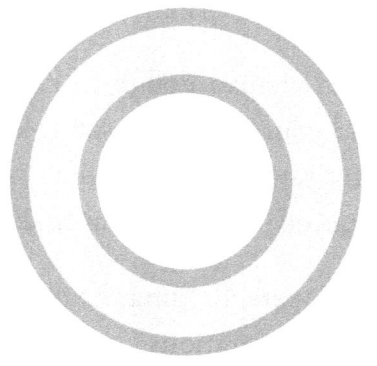

1 JUMP

Taking a day off from my job, I went for the interview. I reached the office around 11 am as instructed. It was located 17 kms from my house, in a place called Aundh, at the other end of Pune. I changed 2 buses and walked almost a kilometer to make it to the venue. That wasn't enough, when I reached the office; I realized that there were nine candidates waiting, including me.

"Hi, I have come for the interview" I said to the security guard manning the reception.

"Can I have your CV?" he asked in a weird tone.

I gave him what he needed and he asked me to join the gang of boys who was waiting for their turn. There were a series of rounds, which we had to go through, and as for the starving exercise most of us faced; we were not offered anything except water. There was no canteen nearby; in fact, none of us could afford to take a chance of going out, and missing out on our turn.

Finally! The time came when I was called in at 6 pm, 7 hours and 10 minutes after my arrival, to be precise. I entered the cabin of Mr. Kartikeyan Bose, the head of marketing. He was a big fat man, sitting on his chair, like a huge creature waiting for its prey. However, he proved otherwise, as we went along.

"Why do you want to join us?" he asked.

"Because I want to change my job," was the quick reply from my side.

"You have worked for just 4 months, and now you want to change your job?" he fired his second question, after running through my CV, which consisted of eight lines on one single page, and a majority of those lines were my address and my hobbies.

"I am fed up with the job; it's monotonous." I answered.

"What if you leave our organization as well, after a few months?" he continued.

"If the job has nothing new in it, then maybe, yes, I will," I said bluntly.

The session went on for more than 35 minutes; it involved some personal and some professional talk. He educated me about the firm and its future prospects, I was sure I scored well in my personal conversation, unlike the professional one. Once I was through, I realized he was happy with me.

"Can you come down tomorrow at 10 am for second round of the interview?" he asked.

"As long as I don't have to wait for the whole day," I said and smiled.

He smiled and said, "You won't, we will be done with you tomorrow at the time you entered today."

I smiled and left bidding him good bye.

Next day I went at 0940, again taking a day off from my work. I went through the sessions and finished by 4, with the offer letter in my hand.

"Congratulations," said Mr. Bose.

"Thank you" I smiled still gazing at the offer letter. I was more excited because the salary offered was 4k and incentives.

I went home and shared this good news with my family. My father wasn't home, as it was still 5.30 in the evening.

"Eehoo! I got the job mom," I screamed.

"Oh, that's great," Mom replied.

My sisters joined the party; they were happy too. I promised I would get them a nice gift once I began this job. We fought like mad dogs, but our love for each other was very strong. This was because they always saved me from dad, when we used to have a heated argument. Besides, they helped me connect with my girl-friends in college. During those days we only had a land line phone, and they were my message-keepers if any of my girl-friends called.

"So when shall we go shopping?" they asked.

"Hey, let me get my salary first!"

Mom was a bit unhappy when she heard about where my office was located. She was worried about my traveling. But I managed to convince her.

Next day, I resigned from the clearing house company, where I worked for just 4 months. I was to join the new office in a week's time. Thank God!

There was nothing then like having to give 2 months' notice, as it is today.

I joined the new office. I just loved the atmosphere. Big office, gigantic terrace, dining hall and as it was a field job, I used to be in the field, most of the time. Mr. Bose was a cool guy to work with, unlike my previous boss and most of the other colleagues as well. There was one similarity between both, my previous boss and Mr. Bose. They were both heavy duty, big fat guys. I was scared if I would become the same once I became a manager which I knew I would never become; I mean the Manager. I thought this FAT all around your body comes with the designation.

I didn't realize when those 6 months passed by. One day I was called in the MD's cabin. Kartikeyan was there as well.

"You were born and raised in Belgaum right?" the MD asked.

"Yes," I replied, wondering what he wanted to do with my place of birth. I thought he was going to fire me for being born there. As Belgaum had been a hot topic for 50 years in Indian history as to which state it belonged to - Maharashtra or Karnataka, still undecided.

"Do you have any relatives there?" he asked.

"My Granny and my aunt live there."

"Over to you Kartikeyan," MD handed over and left the cabin with hisphone.

I was still wondering what was to come as I looked at my MD walking away through the door.

He in turn smiled at me as he made an exit.

"See Nikhil, we are opening up with the biggest HUB center in Belgaum in March, 2001. That is next month. We are looking for someone whom we can trust and who is capable of handling it." Kartikeyan explained.

I did not know what was happening, so I just went ahead and gave a nod to what he said, looking at him helplessly.

"We see a great potential in you and would expect you to handle that center," he continued.

Now that's what shocked me and at the same time gave me a bit of a breather as well. I had worked there for 6 months; time had passed; however, I had made no impact on my company that I knew. But I did not know something had happened and it was this big.

"It is one of the biggest digital libraries in India," he continued.

I was happy that my company believed this much in me. I felt puffed up, like a hot-air balloon, ready to be left in the open sky. And as they say, a small motivation is big enough to get someone to kill himself. That's what happened with me. I was so pumped up that I accepted the offer. My salary was doubled, with the designation of a center manager. Moreover, I had 4 subordinates who reported to me, besides a bonanza waiting for me there.

My family was happy, and so was I, except for my dad. The best part was that I was going to the city, where I had spent my childhood. With some "Yes" and "no", my dad gave me a go ahead and bought a bike too for me; Hero Honda –Splendor in my favorite color black. There was a very sour relationship between dad and me. There was an awkward silence between us always, but then we still loved each other. I believe that is how, most father-son relationships are. I was very happy on seeing the bike.

"Thank you Dad, very sweet surprise," I said.

Dad was in a bit of a serious mood and said, "You are welcome son. In fact, I got this bike for you to go to your office here. As I thought it's hectic to travel by the erratic and inefficient public transport."

I guessed that he had gifted me the bike, but was not completely happy with my decision to leave home. My head went down, as he was looking straight into my eyes.

"But then I heard; this bike has got an excellent mileage. You can travel from Belgaum to Pune at hardly any cost," he said. Then, with a slight pause he added, "Every day."

I looked up; he had a smile on his face. I went close to him, hugged him, which is when I felt the warmth of his love for me. I was so wrong; I realized that. But I had one question, why on earth, do all parents wear that mask of being strict, when they are so caring about their kids deep down, inside? Everyone was absolutely stunned after seeing this drastic change, full-on love between me and dad. And all of them had tears in their eyes. Similar scenes to what I am sure we have seen in quite a lot of Hindi films.

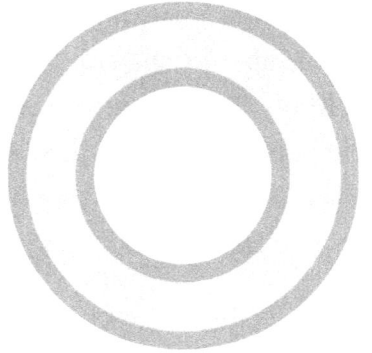

1 SHIFT

Finally, the day came, 28th of February 2001, when I moved to Belgaum. This job re-united me with my granny and aunt. I was raised by them until I moved to Pune when I was 15. Dad, being in the army, had to move from town to town and I was kept with my granny and aunt in Belgaum so that my education was not interrupted. Post-retirement, Dad decided to settle down in Pune. The town has 60% retired citizens. That is the reason why Pune seems to be so secure. I believe he might have just followed suit without much of thinking as most defense personnel seem to do once they retire - "Think less."

My cousins were in a celebratory mood after my arrival. There were about 4 of them. Moreover, my best friend Manik lived there too, my school time buddy. He was senior to me, but we were great pals. He was one of the lucky guys, who resembled Hrithik Roshan, I am not kidding; he did. We called him Hrithik. Every girl wanted to know him and spend some time with him. For them, he was no less than a Chhota Roshan. Blue eyes, same hair style, same face but yes, there was a slight difference; he had a nice pot belly. That's what differentiates Mr. Roshan from Chhota Roshan.

I used to visit this town once a year during the Ganapati festival. Now, coming home permanently with a job was fun, so all of them were happy to see me back in the place where I belonged.

March 1st 2001, I went to college; I mean my new office, Jawahar Lal Nehru Medical College (JNMC) in a nice formal shirt and a trousers. I have never liked this formal wear but when you work you have to do things which you hate the most and today being the opening ceremony I had to. Kartikeyan had told me that it would be a casual atmosphere, though. JNMC is one of the best colleges in Karnataka. It is known for its huge campus, medical syllabus, and as a well-known hub for all the guys from Belgaum who come looking for hot girls.

Everyone had gathered at the venue. It was inaugurated by the Chairman and hundreds of students had flocked there, trust me that was heaven. I mean the center from inside was the talk of the college for months. The whole scene looked like the 8th wonder had been discovered. Everyone's mouth and eyes were open; whispering was heard aloud as it came from every person. I was introduced to all the authorities as the point of contact.

"He is Nikhil, our Center Manager," Kartikeyan introduced me to the Principal of the college.

"Hi, Nikhil! Nice to meet you, Make sure every student and everyone entering here is happy. In case of any problems do call me," said the Principal scanning me from head to toe while handing over his visiting card.

"Sure Sir, please be rest assured," I said.

The library was a huge set up of 60 computers. It was really one of the biggest in India. The money that had been spent on it was six million rupees. Oh la la!!! It had been spent wisely on the interiors and furniture, not to mention the computers and the internet connection. There was a huge beige coloured couch right in front of the reception counter, for the visitors to sit at ease and two glass paneled cabins. It was like a big open hall where tables were set and computers placed very artistically. One could sit in any corner and see the other corner without any strain. The word which came to mind and which I kept on hearing throughout the day from every visitor was "Beautiful!" after visiting this place.

When everyone left and as we started operating, my boss Kartikeyan took me to my cabin.

ONE LOVE

"This is your cabin, Nikhil," he said.

I had never thought one of the 2 cabins would be mine, wow!!!

"And that's your chair," he added as I was looking around.

"Wow!" I whispered as I sunk into the executive chair.

He opened his laptop while I sat on my chair trying to adjust it. He opened a presentation, and asked me to pay attention.

"This is what we are looking for, Nikhil" he said.

"Around 30K for the first month," he said, making it clear.

He took me through the entire presentation, and we finished with the month long plan and all the logistics.

"Hope you liked your new Den," he said as he shut his laptop.

"This is amazing, awesome" I replied.

Meanwhile, he packed his laptop and put all the necessary paperwork in his hand bag. I went to drop him to the hotel Ramdev where he was putting up, hardly 100 meters from the college. He changed and opened a bag full of antibiotics after reaching the room, while I was leafing through a magazine. The pills looked like teeny-weeny toys for a new-born baby in different sizes and shapes. He said he was suffering from backache, and loads of complimentary illnesses, which his marketing tours gave him.

"Everyone is banking on you," he said, as he was swallowing the pills and pushing them down with water into his big fat round tummy. He was wearing a night T-shirt which I had never seen before, since I only saw him wearing formals. Now I was sure he had such a huge pot belly because all the medicines were stored in there, you see.

I said confidently, "I will live up to it."

I was anxious to know more about the medicines, so I asked him "What are these tablets for?"

To that he replied "Oh these, they are my saviors."

"You see I keep on traveling so much that I miss out on home food, and on top of that the travel takes a toll on me," he whined.

I knew where he was heading next; he could open up a big pharmacy if he continued working like this for five more years.

Meanwhile, his dinner came as he had to finish in time to catch a bus for Bangalore where his next assignment waited.

"I will take your leave now," I said getting up from the sofa.

"No, wait have some dinner with me," he suggested as the steward made some place to keep the food with the medicines on the center table. The waiter too was surprised to see so many medicines.

"No thank you, please carry on," was my reply as I was excited to begin my work there at the center.

"Sure?" he questioned to which I responded immediately, "Yes I am."

To that he said, "Then go ahead and handle your throne. And yes, stay away from the women there" he smiled.

I just smiled back and let him continue with his meal and left for the library. I entered the library; I saw it was packed with loads of girls and boys. As I entered, my subordinate Sachin directed their attention towards me for the queries they had. And I was more than happy to answer them. This is the bonanza I had been talking about. The college had a strength of around 2300 students. And trust me; I thought the majority of them were girls. Oh, might be it was me who was vouching for more girls. Can't help it, I was just 23 then. I did entertain queries from the guys, too. I mean, don't take me literally, I was not only answering their queries but being good to them. I never wanted them to get angry enough with me on the first day and hit me for hitting on their college property, you see.

This is how it all started. One incident, which I will always remember is when a girl called Pamela, came to me.

"Hi, I am Pamela" she said.

Trust me; she was a miniature version of Pamela A. Hot with the right assets at the right places.

"Hi I am Nikhil, Nikhil Ranade," said I in Bond style and bowed down and shook her hand.

"This is a wonderful place," she complimented.

I was sure these pretty girls had been taken into consideration while making this place the way it was.

"Oh, yes it is. But less wonderful then you," I acknowledged.

She looked straight into my eyes when she said "Oh, Thank you, but we just met and how can you say that in a moment"

"Wow! Look at you, you hottie. Haven't you stood in front of a mirror before? Or are there no smart men around?" was supposed to be my next card, but then I decided not to do so on the first day and the first meeting.

I settled for, "It takes just a glance to know what is what."

She was as confused as I was. At the same time, her friends came up to us after a proper inspection of the entire place. She introduced me to her friends, who kept on smiling as their names were called out. "This is Fiona, Melinda, Melissa and Jacob," she said. He was the only man among the ladies. I felt a bit jealous, but pacified myself by saying he might be gay, which is what he looked like. All the girls were smoking hot. This is what we say, isn't it, if there is a bunch full of good looking girls, and a single guy, we come to the conclusion that he is just the sibling of one of them.

"Hi guys! It's a pleasure meeting you," I said. In a chorus they just nodded as if they had springs attached to their heads which made them shake at one go.

Meanwhile, Pamela said, "We are all from Goa."

Wow, was my reaction as Goa is just 110 Km from Belgaum. My respect and attraction for that place grew immediately, but had to slow down as they bid goodnight to me. They left as it was almost 9 and as the girls' hostel would close at 9 sharp. So in a few minutes all the ladies were out and the lonely men inside the library were taking away all the charm of the place. I went on talking to some of them, made some friends and later closed the library for the day and went home.

I reached home at around 11.45 pm. As my Granny and aunt were asleep, I ate my dinner and hit the cot.

"A good start after all, Nikhil, way to go!" is what I said to myself looking at the roof. I inspired myself and slept thinking about Pamela and the beaches of Goa.

1 DREAM

Next day when I woke up, I wasn't on the beaches of Goa, but on the floor kissing the dust and Pamela wasn't beside me but my granny, who asked me, "What happened, son?"

I looked at my granny, rubbed my eyes and wiped the sticky saliva from the edges of my mouth. Yuck, that's when I realized why men are addressed as dogs by women.

"Oh, nothing Aayi, what's the time and how come I fell down?" I asked her.

"I guess it is 5.45 am and all I know is I heard a loud bang. It must have been your head banging on the floor. But what happened to you?" she inquired.

How could I tell her that I had been dreaming of Goa and those lovely girls?

I slowly got up and sat on the bed holding my head which was hurting.

There was a pain somewhere else as well, I guess I fell down on that, I mean my stomach.

"I believe it's the work pressure" I said trying to avoid eye contact running my hand slowly down there and making some important adjustments.

She gave me a pat on my shoulder. "Sleep for some more time. What time do you have to be at work?" she asked.

"Yes I will, I have to leave by 9," I replied.

I drew the sheet over me and went back to sleep again. This time I surely wanted to be in my senses while asleep. I prayed to God that I don't want to be in the same situation again. In no time I was fast asleep.

Suddenly, I felt a hand on my cheeks caressing me. This time it was no dream but reality and guess what, my Aunt was asking me to get up. I woke up.

"It's 8 am, get up Nikhil" said my aunt.

"It's 8 o'clock," I repeated.

My aunt looked stunned; she must have been thinking that I was already out of my senses. She was looking at me in a funny way.

"Yes it is 8, get up," my granny added.

My aunt was a real comic; I thought she might be playing a prank on me. But this time she was serious. I was wondering what was wrong if I had paraphrased her question. In fact, the reason why that happened was told to me later.

Granny had told her that I had fallen on the ground head on. Haa! Now I know why she looked at me like that.

"I heard a loud bang and when I came here, he had fallen on the ground!"

My granny told my aunt, laughing while she got a hot cup of tea for me.

I too had a wicked smile on my face as I took the cup from granny.

"How was your first day?" My aunt inquired.

"It was very good," I answered.

We all made small talk and then I left with my black beauty. I had driven down my bike to Belgaum, with the help of my cousin Ninad - the youngest and the cutest of my cousins. Ninad was into bike modification, and used to help his dad in the garage which they managed for 2 wheelers.

I reached my office at 9 sharp as it was 4 kilometers from my house. I had been given the job of opening and closing the main door too. I believe modern-day managers also have to keep a check on their library, especially if it's a digital one. Anyway, my subordinate was already there, his name was Sachin. He was from Belgaum, a sweet looking kid, he might have been almost my age, but his mind was that of a ten year old boy.

"Give me the keys, I will open," he proposed.

I handed him the keys, He opened the lock. May be I forgot to mention, the digital Library was in a huge building which used to be their original college library.

And now a part of that library was used by us. So there was a main entrance for the building which used to open at 8 and then another entrance for my den. Hope you have gotten how it was placed.

We both entered and started all the computers. Slowly students started coming, and I started to interact with them. Some of them wanted to get a membership card which we promised to give them at a discount. However I was expecting a technician to come from Pune and install the software so that the membership system could be started. All the schemes and upcoming packages were put on a huge notice board right next to the couch opposite to the reception.

Time passed by and it was 11:30 am. At that time I was sitting next to Sachin, a lady walked in with her daughter wearing an apron, or let me call it a lab coat. They observed the whole library and came to Sachin. "Who is in charge here?" she asked. To that Sachin looked at me, and I in turn stood up.

"What can I do for you Ma'am?" I said.

"What is the membership for this place?" she asked.

"Ma'am, we have not started with the membership as yet."

"You may sooner or later do that, right?" she threw another statement at me.

"Yes, we will, but that would take some time," I replied.

"So how much is it going to be?" she demanded.

"It has not been planned yet," I answered politely.

She had another query in her kitty. "How much do you charge per hour?"

"Fifteen rupees, Ma'am."

"Wow, that's quite cheap. In Bombay, if you want to browse, it is sixty bucks" she said looking at her daughter, who was a mute spectator with her mother doing all the talking until then. They looked so happy as if they had struck gold in a savings competition. I was dumbstruck looking at their expression, and embarrassed at the same time as Sachin was

31

looking at me with a blank face.

"She is my daughter, Ruta. Whenever you start with your membership scheme please get her enrolled," was the last statement she mouthed.

They both left. And we continued our business as usual. In the evening Ruta came to the library at 08:30 pm.

"Hi, I am sorry for the session in the morning," she said, pleadingly.

"No worries. That's my job."

"I am Ruta Bhatkande," she said with a smile on her face.

Meanwhile, I extended my hand saying, "I am Nikhil, Nikhil Ranade." Exactly in the style of... I am sure you guessed it right. "And he is Sachin."

She told me that she was in her 1st year of BDS (Bachelor in Dental surgery).

"I guessed it," I said "with that beautiful smile on you."

She smiled and thanked me in return. She was a very ordinary girl but a sophisticated one, with a beautiful smile and the right blend of attitude. I told her that I was from Pune and we became friends.

1 MUSIC

With all these introductions happening, I was the topic of the college for my flirtatious talk, and my friendly nature. All the girls were on my wish list.

Everyone started to be friendly and I started to know them. I set up a pair of speakers in the library.

"Do you think it's the right place for the speakers?" I asked Sachin, as we made some place for the music.

I started playing music softly as per everyone's request. I knew which song was whose favorite. There was one song, which happened to be my favorite too, that went "Smack my bitch up." Guess what? This was the one which Pamela liked and then I started liking it too. I was sure all the guys wanted a piece of her, but I wanted her completely. Whenever I used to play this song, she used to turn around or get up from wherever she was sitting, give me a thumbs up and a wink. Oh, let me tell you, I used to play it only when she was around, not otherwise.

It was not only she, but almost all the members used to come to me and request their songs, I used to download the songs for them and play them whenever they came in. It was a different atmosphere altogether. I started sitting next to Sachin rather than in my cabin, I was more of a DJ and a public relation officer than a Center Manager, but that really paid off for me. In fact, this friendly nature saved me and my company from the disadvantage of the internet connection, which was horrifyingly slow sometimes. It was a lease line and supposed to be Jet fast; however, it was slower than the USB connections that we get today. Users at the library used to calm down just because of me, and the rapport I started building with them. Days passed by, and I realized that I had started loving this job and the people around, but oh, not in that way.

One day i.e. in the third week a guy called Asif came to me, he was from Bombay.

"You are a womanizer man. (In Bambaaiya language you call it CHAMDI, a very low and cheap sounding word, that's why I wanted to ignore it) Hats off to you," he said

34

"What did I do"? I asked him with anxiety, wondering what he knew about me. I was wondering if he knew more than he should have. He had a wicked grin on his face.

"Saw you at the Panchvati lodge on Sunday....with a beautiful girl," he said.

I just smiled and kept quiet. By now, everyone in the college knew about my Casanova image, as I was seen with the ladies almost all the time and that too in just a few weeks' time.

He leaned close with a smile and introduced himself.

"I need a machine for an hour," Asif said to Sachin.

He took a machine and I sat beside him. As we chatted for more than an hour, I found most of our likes matched. The music, the game and of course we both loved women. But the difference was, I used to get them and he used to want them. He was tall, dark and an average guy.

"Man, I really want to know the techniques for attracting women," he said.

"There are no techniques, its pure spontaneity and confidence," I replied.

I believed that, all one needs to attract a woman, is being confident and spontaneous, besides being persuasive of course.

We became friends, and he used to stay late browsing and

chatting with us - me, Sachin, and another colleague Gagan, who was our technician. We used to call Gagan, Tukki, a Hindi-cised word for Techie. Gagan was a simple person, from a small town with big dreams in his eyes. He used to stay late sometimes, and go through various sites and download study material. I hoped he was not watching porn. I should agree that, sometimes I broke the rule of keeping the center closed and locking it myself.

Slowly the first month passed, and I realized, that the target was achieved and way beyond. It's not only that but I even realized that I had never been as happy as this before. However, as they say, nothing is constant. The only thing constant is change. But does that change, change constantly? May be!

One day I received a call in the library office. The clerk came up to me and summoned me.

"Nikhil, there is a call for you," he said.

"Who is it"? I asked him.

"Someone from Pune, I guess," he said and left immediately. I walked behind him. I had to walk almost 50 meters to get the phone. In 2001, there were hardly any cell phones, and if there were, using them for a single long call was like emptying your pocket to the tune of a month's fuel in your bike. Fuel prices were Rs. 22/- and every call cost was Rs. 16/- per minute. That's not all, incoming calls were charged too. Moreover, we had no phone in the digital library - that was the only thing which we lacked in our set up. I wanted to say to my Boss that we had spent Rs. 6 million, but couldn't get a phone connection worth Rs. 600/- Any ways, I grabbed the receiver.

"Hello," I said.

"Hey Nikhil! Awesome job. I just returned from Delhi and saw the collections for the 1st month. Rajnish is very proud of you," Kartikeyan on the other side was overjoyed saying all this in one single breath.

"It's been my pleasure, Sir," was my reply.

"I am coming to Belgaum, and will catch up with you," he said.

"Sure, Sir" with an eager voice I uttered.

"Now, I am least worried about the Belgaum center" was his last statement. I hung the phone up, and saw the librarian who was sitting there with a pile of files in front of him. Vacations were over, and college had just started. May be, he was enrolling the new students.

"Hello Mr. Krishnamurthy, how are you"? I greeted him.

"I am fine Nikhil, how are you?" he asked.

"I am doing fine, hope to get a phone line in the center, sorry for the trouble" I apologized.

"No, no don't say that, you are always welcome here. In fact, I wanted to thank you for that day when you helped me with the power point presentation," he said.

"Oh, I am honored, Sir," I said and smiled. He had come up to me one day and asked for help in making a presentation for the development in the library.

I wished him good day and returned back. As soon as I entered, I saw everyone getting up and leaving their respective places. They were all at the cash counter.

"What happened, Sachin?" I inquired.

"The net is down," he said. Net being down was an ordinary thing but it used to get fixed in a few minutes, unlike this time.

"So where is Gagan? Ask him to fix it up," I suggested.

Meanwhile, Gagan popped out from the router room, dusting his hands with a kilo of dust flying around, which he had managed to collect while shifting the router.

"The problem is with the service provider," he said. "We have to contact the BSNL office."

Meanwhile, all the students started to wind up their work and leave. Sachin and I both apologized for the inconvenience and let them go. That problem took 3 working days to be rectified, and during the process I learnt that, managing a library was not just sweet talking to women or being friends with the staff, it was more than that, and that thing was to liaise with the BSNL people as well. Who, like all our government employees, are laid back with the attitude of Ho jaayega, which never happens. All they want to do is, come, sign-in for the day in the roster, and warm up the chairs for 5 hours as they spend 3 hours loitering around out of 8 hours' duty. But any way, I kept on learning things, as we all do in every walk of life. There is always a roller coaster ride in life, just face it and try to enjoy the lows as well. We were getting used to it.

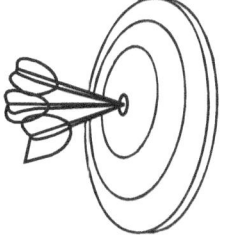

1 ENCOUNTER

One and a half months passed by, with good collections and great reports, we were all set with perfect revenues. Almost 3 times more than what was expected. We were in the month of April; I was sitting next to Sachin talking to him and discussing the shift change which he was looking for. Our other employee Pallavi, who used to work from 11pm to 6am, wanted a morning shift. I am sorry I never mentioned her. She was one out of five from our team, and the last one was Assistant Technician Ranga. He was an enthusiastic guy, in his early 20s. He used to assist Gagan in all the technical aspects.

So, we were discussing the change, when a girl walked up to the counter with one more friend of hers. She came to Sachin and paid for both of them.

"How much is it?" she asked.

"It's thirty, Saloni," Sachin said after checking her login time. He knew her name so he just had to see the login hours.

"Take the money for Zainab as well," she said, after handing over a 100 rupee note.

Meanwhile, there was another friend of theirs', who came and paid for herself. Zainab was a thin girl with a funny smile who was from Bombay. Whenever she used to speak, she used to animate in style. Her hands would go up and down, her mouth would open wide as per the intensity of the situation and her eyes would pop out with every gesture she made. The third was Priyanka. Priyanka was a big mama but cute like a doll. If someone saw her walking from behind, they would feel that a polar bear was walking, wearing a Salwaar Kameez, which she usually wore. I am sure; there wouldn't be a size of jeans for her. Saloni was cute, with a beautiful smile and a very average girl. An average girl meaning; a girl who was not as thin as Zainab or as huge as Priyanka, nor did she have outstanding looks and wasn't bad either. Whatever she was, she didn't attract me.

Any ways, Zainab came to Sachin and asked him if he could download a song for her. He said yes.

"Which song is it, Sachin?" I asked.

He said "You are my sunshine."

"Wow, that's a nice song," I said appreciatively and smiled.

She blushingly said "You too like it?"

"It's a good song, a good song is a good song you see" I answered. Saloni came to me and introduced herself finding an opportunity.

"Hi, I am Saloni," she said with an innocent smile spread across her face.

I stood up and introduced myself, in my usual style.

She introduced her friends to me. "She is Zainab, and she is Priyanka."

They both smiled and shook hands. Meanwhile, Asif entered and logged in.

While passing by he said "I have mailed you some stuff do check it."

I gave him a nod. I gave a look at these girls standing next to me, and got my eyes glued on to Saloni. I didn't notice that may be I was thinking something else.

Saloni in the meanwhile asked me "Can I have your email address? I will mail you some good forwards," she said, having a much bigger smile this time, with an excitement.

I looked at her and glanced at everyone, and replied "Saloni, don't mind, but we have just met, and I don't give my email to everyone." I was saying it as if I was Pierce Brosman, who does not want unnecessary fan followers. She didn't say anything, her smile withered as she stood for some time, while Zainab was busy with Sachin for some more song requests, and they left.

With a disappointment on her face she walked out from there. I didn't see it but Sachin noticed it. Sachin was a guy whose ears were all open, to catch any flying news or gossip. Looks are deceptive, I completely agree. As they left, Sachin voiced out something which I never knew.

"She comes every day at this time, sits for 2 hours at the same place," he pointed out the place where she found herself comfortable.

That place was right next to my cabin. My cabin was immediately right after the entrance. If we walked a few more steps, the router room was straight ahead. It was like an "H" shaped set up. My cabin used to come right in the middle. She used to sit behind my cabin, from where she could see through my glass paneled windows and see me, even if I was at Sachin's place or anywhere else. After a bit of scratching, I mean my brain, I asked Sachin, "So what do I do?"

"I don't know, I am just informing you, that she is regular, never talks too much, but is always in a happy mood unlike today when she left," he replied.

I didn't pay attention to what he said, and continued with the day. From my point of view, I was innocent and right, and when you think that way, the whole world turns out to be WRONG.

Few days passed, I was busy filing some reports in my cabin, and then I heard a knock on my door and saw it was Zainab and Priyanka.

"Hey come in," I invited them, inviting trouble for myself. As they walked in I asked them to sit. "Take a seat, please." Zainab came straight to the point in defense of her friend.

"Nikhil we are here for a favor from you, it may sound stupid, but that's how it is," she began.

"What are you talking about," I inquired surprised, stopping doing what I was doing.

"We are talking about our friend Saloni," Priyanka replied looking at Zainab and then at me.

No matter what happens, true friends are always there for you.

"She is acting weird, not attending lectures, doesn't eat food," Zainab added as her decibel level went up.

"So what can I do about that?" I demanded, getting one hand under my chin and the other on the handle of the chair. Same as the big B would do, if he was to ask "KITNEY

AADMI THE?" (Please note – this is Amjad Khan's dialogue, not Amitabh's. Please replace with some other line.)

"That's what we are requesting you, just be her friend," Zainab suggested, as if all the strength and breath she had gathered was utilized and now she shrunk into the chair.

"But, why?" was my question, as I leaned ahead with anger.

"Because she likes you."

I interrupted Zainab, "Wait, what did you say?" Now that's when my volume went up.

"She likes you, I said" repeated Zainab in a composed manner.

I was surprised and amused by this, with a funny laugh on my face.

"Do you know that she has been coming here for over a month now?"

Priyanka said.

"And you know why she comes here? Just to have a glimpse of you," she added.

Zainab immediately added "Have you ever heard a girl saying, I love the way he flirts with the girls, the way he speaks to them, have you ever heard that?"

I was shocked, as I never heard these things before. I was

mentally numb, and was just watching them and trying to gather whatever they were saying. Moreover, my eyes started wandering all over the place through the glasses that masked my cabin.

Finally, Zainab finished by saying "Please, it's a request; she may be ok in a few weeks. Just pretend to be her friend and be good to her."

Zainab and her friend Priyanka sounded more mature, than Saloni or any girl of that age. They were just 19, in the first year of their Physiotherapy College after 12th, which Priyanka never looked like. But I guess, whenever you see someone in difficulty, you happen to be the master and when you get into it, you falter.

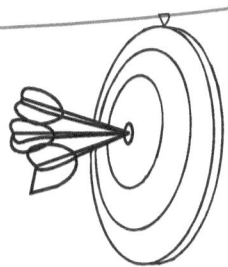

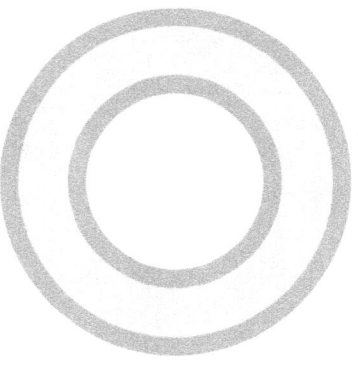

1 POEM

Few days passed by, it was May 2nd 2001. I stepped out of my cabin with some reports and was having a discussion with Sachin, at the cash counter.

It was around 7pm; meanwhile, Saloni came to the counter. She looked at me and I glanced at her. The words of her friends echoed in my ears.

"Pretend to be a friend to her, she will be alright in few weeks." Sounds very filmi but yes, that's what happened. Sachin gave her the change back and she was leaving.

"Thank you Saloni," said Sachin, as he was trying to make up for what I had done a few weeks ago. She took the money and turned around to leave.

"Hey Saloni how are you?" I said.

She stopped and replied "I am fine, thank you Nikhil." She elaborated on the latter part of her sentence, may be to make me realize.

"You are fine! Doesn't look like," I triggered.

"Just a bit of studies, nothing much" she said.

Meanwhile, Zainab walked towards the counter. She was happy seeing us talking.

"Hi Sachin, how much do I pay?" she asked Sachin.

"Forty-five," said Sachin.

Meanwhile Priyanka stepped inside. All the 3 musketeers were dressed to the kill.

"So where are you headed?" I asked looking at all of them and freezing on Saloni.

Priyanka was over-excited to say "To the Ice Cream parlour!"

"Why don't you join us Nikhil?" Zainab continued.

"Oh no. I need to be here," was my reply.

To that, my sweet pal Sachin had to interfere. "Hey Boss,

why don't you go, I will manage." Now I realized his ears were truly everywhere. He didn't even mind turning around 180 degree, stretching his head high up and making an effort.

"Ya ya why not, any ways, it will take just 30 minutes," Priyanka calculated.

I was about to say something when Saloni interrupted me, "Don't force someone girls. Let's go."

"Ok, let's go" Priyanka and Zainab said in harmony.

I thought it was just a small walk outside and 30 minutes, won't do much harm. And before they left I got up and said, "Hey girls wait, I am joining you."

There was a mild smile on Saloni's face, and when I looked at her and smiled, it didn't increase.

We made our way through the library and stepped outside. Ok, let me tell you what the outside of my library looked like. There was a small garden, and a temple right opposite the library. And few meters away, we had a 2 wheeler parking, and a road which if taken left was towards the exit of the college and the other obviously inside. So we took left towards the exit and started walking. We all walked in a single line occupying the whole road. The order was Saloni, Zainab, Priyanka and me.

Zainab opened up the talking account "Nikhil, please do

something about the net speed ya." If there was any Big Boss of Bakwaas, she would have been crowned.

Priyanka immediately seconded the motion "Yeah, it's pathetic."

I just kept on nodding, neither did Saloni add any value to their talks.

The discussion on the internet connection went on for about 4 minutes, and that's when Saloni spoke.

Saloni voiced her views too by adding "The worst part is, when you sit for almost fifteen twenty minutes over an email, and then when you send it, it gets disconnected, that's the bad side and the worst part is to retype it again".

"What do you do for 15 – 20 minutes on an email" I asked anxiously. "I hope you don't write to President Bush," I pulled her leg and we all started laughing.

She frowned staring at everyone and we stopped laughing.

"Any ways, do you all visit this ice cream parlor frequently?" I inquired to change the topic.

"It has just opened," said Zainab.

Priyanka started sharing her experience, with the ice cream the day before. "When me and Fiona, we were returning from our visit from the stationary shop. We saw this place, they had just inaugurated it. When we tried, my god it was yummmm." Loads of mmm she used, to describe the sweet taste of that ice cream.

Zainab asked me "Do you like ice creams Nikhil?"

"Not much into it, but there is nothing which I don't like to eat if served in front of me," I said.

"Which flavour do you like?" Saloni asked.

"Oh, me? I like bottle gourd" I replied and everyone started laughing again.

"How funny," she said and walked ahead while we kept on laughing at her.

We reached the place with a short conversation about ice creams. Guess what? The place was closed, as there was a short circuit in the parlor, the workers in the outlet informed us. Wow, what a time for a short circuit to happen. That means, I may have to come with them again, good God save me, was my inner voice saying to me.

All of us turned back disappointed. The reason for me getting disappointed was different though. These girls wanted to take me to some other place, I declined. So they too started back to the college premises with me.

Meanwhile, Saloni asked me "So where are you from Nikhil?"

"Pune."

"Oh, MH 12 is Pune?"

What? was my immediate response.

"Your bike's number MH 12," she said.

I realized her friends were right about her. I understood and didn't get deeper into it.

"Oh," I replied and kept quiet.

To that, she told me that she was from Miraj, a 3 hour journey from Belgaum, which she frequently visited over the weekends.

She threw another question to me, as we were heading back to the premises as if we were in a park walking under the moonlight "So what do you do other than working here."

I happily answered "I listen to loads of music and write."

"Write!" she shouted loudly, "Wow, I also write!"

"Oh that's nice!"

I was an amateur writer, but had a habit of boasting about my writing and this time I was in trouble. When all this was happening, her friends were ahead of us having their own talks. Hope they were not discussing some massive plan for internet connectivity which they are capable of designing, any plans which are rubbish.

"What do you write?" Saloni asked me.

"Poems and songs."

"Wow, I write poems too. One of my poems was selected for a prize in the US," she said. She named the website as poettree.com.

I was not amazed, as they select any poem for competition, just to get the entries, making money through some emotional people like us.

She started to recite the poem......And trust me it was really sweet like her.

After she finished, I wanted to present one of my creation as well.

"Hey girls, listen, come here, he is reciting one of his poems" she said to those ladies Einstein.

I went ahead and did the same. They all loved it. Meanwhile we reached the college near my library building. Before we could leave for our respective dens, that is, their hostel and my make-shift house my digital library. Saloni put herself in a spot.

"Hey Nikhil, can we go for a drive sometime," she proposed.

I was frozen and looked at her, and then at her friends, who were distant from us again. I believe they were trying to give us some privacy.

"No Saloni, sorry to tell you but that would be too much to ask."

Her head went down as she said "No issues Nikhil, thank you for coming with us. Bye."

All of them waved bye to me and left.

I went into the center, forgot about the evening and wound up late as usual.

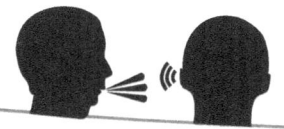

1 ADVICE

It was a weekend and most of the weekends happened to be empty, because all the students used to go to watch movies on these days. That being the only recreation in Belgaum. No night clubs, no pubs, bowling, carting nothing at all. And being a non-peak day I invited my friend Manik to the center and decided to go for lunch. He was working with Adarsh Palace one of the best hotels in Belgaum as a Front office manager. As soon as he came, we both headed for a restaurant on my bike.

Hotel Ramdev was close by and had a restaurant bar which was very famous. They had a great name in F&B services. They had lodging as well their rooms were always booked by college students, which I too had used some time ago. The party hall which they had was booked almost every weekend for birthday parties and events. We entered and got into a bar. A good ambience made it a great start. I could see loads of familiar faces sipping down drinks like water. We found a table in the middle, by the time we reached the table I had waved to almost a dozen students.

"And tell me how is the center operating?" Manik started as we settled down.

"It's fantastic, my Bosses are happy, and so am I," I proudly told him scanning through the menu.

"That's great, I want to come to your center during the week days, one day. I am sure most of the guys and girls will know me," he said in a wicked way.

"Ya, why not it's yours, you are always welcome," I invited him.

Meanwhile the waiter came to our table with a fake smile on his face.

Looked as if the bow they tied on the neck had an effect over it. Whenever the smile starting fading away while taking the order, he used to touch it, move it left, right and the smile was back again.

We ordered our drinks and the waiter served it in no time. I was surprised at the service but Manik told me the real reason behind it. There were a number of people waiting for their turn as we entered, the message was loud and clear, finish your food and drinks and take your ass off the bar.

Manik had 2 chilled beers and I had a chilled orange juice. I used to drink beer but then I had to go to the center so chose not to.

I continued asking him, "What do you mean by saying most of the students know you?"

"Oh, most of them spend their weekends at my hotel he said. The majority of business I get is from this college," he added.

"What are you saying?"

He told me the complete story of the students and how they sneaked into his hotel. How hostel girls applied for a week out saying they were visiting their LG (local Guardians). But I was least interested in this as I have never believed in gossip. He even told me; if you want to get someone do let me know. You will get a handsome discount. I knew I was going to get lucky with some of the Goan girls as I had the week before.

"You will be my man," I said making a deal with a high five.

The lunch was served, some nice fish starters and meat in the main course. It was really an awesome lunch. As the lunch proceeded, I told him about Saloni and the way things were going on.

"These medical students are like this, just go ahead have fun and forget it," he said.

To that I explained to him that the situation was looking different. I told him the complete story of what Zainab and Priyanka told me.

"Oh, and how do you know all this?"

"She has 2 best friends, who told me all this and on top of that I can see it. She behaves a bit weird, when I say no to any offers or requests she makes." I told him about the incident which happened the day before. To that this man had something else to say.

"I don't know, but we all have heard this… Love those who love you, don't run behind things which in turn are running behind somebody else. May be just stop, turn around and see if someone is behind you," he finished his long statement.

I could not understand it clearly, but tried to connect all the pieces and realized that, the love factor can give you immense happiness and the lust will keep you wandering for more, unsatisfied with every act. Soon I got into my world of analysis. We were talking but my mind was somewhere else, might be that statement of his was lingering in my head and my heart like the strong Davidoff 'Cool Waters' perfume.

We finished our lunch and headed towards the library. He came in for some time to browse the net. After sometime he was leaving when Zainab walked in. On seeing him she stopped at the counter.

"Hey Nikhil, how are you?" She said, trying to balance her looks between both of us.

"I am good, Zainab and hope you are fine too. You look excited though," I said.

"Oh no, nothing, just came in to chat, I mean browse the net," she explained.

She was still looking at him, so I went ahead and introduced them.

"He is Manik, she is Zainab"

They exchanged smiles, the smile being broader on Zainab's face.

"Will catch you soon," said Manik to me and made an exit.

Zainab went ahead for her usual chat session, and returned after 3 and-a-half-hours to the counter. I was sitting in my cabin with some presentation for my Boss, who was to visit in the coming week. She knocked on my door and came in.

"Hey, Nikhil! Who was that handsome guy?" she said.

I knew there was something fishy, and maybe Manik was right, all the girls want the same thing as the boys do from the "opposite sex", other than a few exceptions which the law has finally considered ethical.

"Who? Manik? He is my friend, why?"

"No, nothing, just like that," she fumbled.

I thought I was already looking at the mess around me and this started getting better. Wow!

"What does he do? Is he from Belgaum?" She fired 2 questions at one go, playing music with her excited fingers on my table.

"He is a Front Office Manager, and yes he is from Belgaum. And single," I answered softly, an additional query which would have come towards me sooner or later. I purposely didn't tell her the name of the hotel, thinking that she might use his hotel room with him being the partner in crime. She was looking at me and her eyes read "GIVE HIM TO me BABY, Ah ha....ah ha." She was definitely the happiest girl on earth for that moment. I don't know why, maybe she had already begun to fantasize about him.

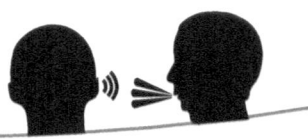

1 WHAT !

Another week passed by and everything was going well. My big Boss made a visit for the first time and appreciated my work. There was no sign of Saloni in the library for quite some time. In fact, one day, on 12th May 2001, I stepped out of the director's office for a short meeting. While returning back, I saw a big group of boys and girls laughing out loud. It was either a session when they might have heard Rajnikant visiting the moon for Dinner or they might have just attended a laughing therapy classes. Whatever the reason was, there was one soul among that huge group which was quiet.

An extreme opposite reaction on her face, as if nothing was happening around. She seemed to be in her own world. She was none other than Saloni. I spotted her and was quite surprised; a girl who is always laughing and cheerful is tight-lipped. Zainab and Priyanka too were having a ball, and Zainab, another character cracking some of her PJ's and laughing so hard at them herself, seemed as if she would fall on the road flat out.

They were all walking towards the hostel, as it was 0230 in the afternoon. I guessed it was lunch time for them. I just went back to my office and believe they went to their hostel. I went up to Reena and told her the minutes of the meeting with the director, and asked her to share it with rest of the colleagues if I was out. The most important of them was the music, which he wanted to stop playing. But I convinced him about playing it; however he negotiated on lowering the volume. In the evening around 6 pm, Zainab walked in and the bombshell Pamela followed her.

"Hi Zainab, how are you?" I greeted.

To that she had a very cold reply "Fine, thank you."

She went towards Sachin, who had come for the evening shift and logged in.

Meanwhile Pamela came towards me.

"Hey Nikhil how are you?" Pamela said.

"I am doing good, Madame," I replied.

"I heard there are going to be loads of changes in your library?" She inquired.

"Nothing much, may be the volume of the music would go a little lower," I said. "It would ask you to sit a bit closer to the counter, where the speakers are kept, closer to me," I said and winked.

She winked back and smiled. I thought I was getting closer to taking her to bed. She went ahead and the song followed as usual. Smack my......up!

After just another fifteen minutes, I thought of talking to Zainab about Saloni. I went up to her.

"Is everything alright with Saloni"?

"Like you care," she said, without even looking at me, staring at the screen.

"I saw you all in the afternoon and found her really low."

She stopped whatever she was doing, and turned around to me and looked up.

"Yes she is not doing well, in fact, she is in a bad phase," she replied, looking straight into my face. "And you know the reason behind this?" she continued.

I was quiet, didn't say a word. I was just looking at her and trying to hear what she was saying.

"It's you, Nikhil," she said, "but I don't blame you for that, as it's her mistake after all," she added.

And what a time it was, that just then Saloni walked in to see if Zainab was there. She located Zainab and saw me with her. But she ignored me somewhat.

"Hey you here, I need your help," she sighed, and sweat was dripping off her face, looking like she had just finished running for a marathon.

"Why what happened?" Zainab inquired.

"I needed some books from the library but I think I have misplaced my library card somewhere," she said. "Can you come with me for five minutes?" she requested Zainab.

"You haven't misplaced your card, but you left your wallet in the lab, dumbo!" Zainab replied. Two dumb people having a conversation in style and proving superior to the other. Zainab took the wallet out and gave it to Saloni.

"Hey so sweet of you, thanks ya," Saloni said.

She took the wallet, and started to leave without even giving me a glance. I was a mute spectator, all this while, just watching all this happening. I didn't know what it was; I followed Saloni as she left and before she could exit the door I stopped her.

"Hey Saloni," I said as she turned around.

"Hi Nikhil," she said with her head almost down and standing right in the middle of the door, which was half open and which she held with her foot.

"Hey what happened to you, long time no see? And whenever I saw you, you seemed to be lost."

"Hey nothing, just a bit of studies and nothing much" she replied and moved aside as there was a visitor at the door.

"Are you sure, it's only studies nothing else?" I dug into it, to know what the matter was.

"Yes nothing much," she faltered while saying it.

"Oh ok. No issues," I paused, "just wanted to see if you had time."

"Time?" Saloni asked with a surprised face.

"Just looking forward to go for a drive with you, but I guess you are busy studying now"

The whole atmosphere changed, her head rose up, a smile stretched her lips and the suppressed voice shot out.

"What?"

But that's what made everyone turn around from whatever they were doing. Sachin was the first person to do so, he turned around to see if I was asking some girl to strip right here right now. The people, whoever was passing by, in and out of the library stopped for a fraction of a second, to see what's happening there? They glanced at me and then at Saloni, which they did a few times until they went out of the library; any ways, the spectators continued their walk.

"I was looking forward to go for a drive with you. It's fine may be next time."

To that she replied with a question and an answer by herself "I will manage my studies, you tell me when are you free, tomorrow at 6pm?"

I was happy to see excitement on her face and her heightened energy level.

"7 tomorrow, will that be fine?" I asked her.

"Yes, yes," she replied.

"But I hope it won't hamper your studies."

"No... no, it won't," she smiled.

"Ok then, see you!" I ended the conversation with a smile.

"Bye," she said and started walking towards the door, in filmi style she turned around and said "Thank you, Nikhil."

I simply smiled at her. As she left I returned to the cash counter. Where an excited Sachin was keen to ask me what happened with that "WHAT" being said so loud.

"Is everything alright Boss?" he asked.

"Yes, nothing"

And I continued the evening as usual, thinking of tomorrow evening.

1 CRUSH

The next day was business as usual. Luckily that week, the internet was not down and there was not much running around. Visiting BSNL once a fortnight for the net connection was normal. The day went by well and I literally forgot that I had a promise in place.

Saloni entered at 55 past 6. I was in my cabin, she smiled at me and went ahead and sat on the couch. After 25 minutes I stepped out of my cabin and saw her sitting there. I smiled and she smiled back. She was dressed in a half sleeves white checks shirt and dark blue denim. There was nothing loud about her make up or dressing - subtle as usual.

"Are we going?" she asked

I was puzzled for a moment.

"Going, where?" Her face turned sad. I wondered if I had said something wrong.

That was an indication for me, and I in no time recovered my words and the promise I made to her.

"Hey, I am just kidding," I said. "How come you are late, we were supposed to go at 7, right?"

"I was here before 7," she replied and started laughing.

"What are you saying, then why didn't you come to me?" I demanded.

"I thought you were busy, so didn't bother to disturb you."

"Hey, I am just kidding, I saw you coming, sorry for the delay. Give me a minute."

She gave a nod to this. I went up to Reena, who filled in for Sachin who had gone for his friend's wedding.

"Reena, I will come in a while, just look after the center in the meantime," I informed her.

"No worries, Boss" Reena replied.

We left the library and stepped out towards my bike. In a few minutes we were out of the college campus. Driving down the road, we left the city limits towards the NH4 which was hardly a km away. There were small hamlets on the edges of the highway. After 10 minutes of driving, Saloni spotted a juice center.

"Hey stop! Stop! Stop! There is a juice center," she said gesturing with her left hand as her head turned behind with the bike being driven ahead.

I had to control a 14 horse(s) power bike to come to a halt. By the time I stopped we were a bit ahead. Wish bikes too had air brakes especially for those who have girl-friends and that too, excited ones. I pulled over in style, and drove on the wrong side for almost 50 meters escaping the heavy vehicles. I stopped the bike in front of the juice stall. She immediately got down as the bike came to a halt. So did I, I put the bike on the stand and turned towards the stall, while Saloni was watching me.

"Hey what happened?" I asked her.

"Nothing," she said and smiled.

As we turned towards the stall, we noticed something unusual or may be for the 1st time. We saw that the menu and the hoarding were the same.

The name "Jai Ganesh" was written in the middle of a rectangular board in an oval shape. And the juices offered were mentioned all around it almost similar font. The rates were mentioned there too.

"I will go for a mango milk shake" I said, without even

running through the offerings. That was the easy option out as I believe it's better to go for what you know and have tasted before, especially when you have to spot something from sheer chaos. Moreover, mango was my favorite.

She looked at the board for some more time rubbing her hand over her jaw, as if she was playing who wants to be a millionaire and she was at the final question.

She stared at the hoarding, oops sorry, the menu card and then finally decided for a strawberry milk shake. I went ahead and brought the respective drinks. She drank it slowly, whereas I finished my shake in a few minutes, she continued for a long time. I had to hold on to my glass, and wait for her to finish so that I could keep it aside. May be the reason why she went slow with it was because she wanted to say so many things. But I began the first show.

"Have you come here before?" I asked her.

"No, you never brought me here," she said and winked.

I smiled at her; she smiled in return and began her talk which I never thought would be so smooth.

"You know, I hardly go out in Belgaum and it has just been 2 months. Anyways, when I am in Miraj, I go out with my brother. He has that nice bike, some weird name I don't remember," she laughed sipping in some more strawberry.

"We go around the whole city in the night, during the Ganapati Festival, I take my dad out and he drives me through."

She went on talking, telling me about her family, her friends, and her friends in JNMC here. She told me that her brother and she were twins. She was talking like a child, so innocent and there was an excitement as well in her voice. I could do nothing but listen to her, and went on admiring every gesture, every move she made. She was like a VJ presenting a show on how to drink a strawberry milk shake "SLOWLY." She was stirring around while talking. She was looking at the sky, pointing at the stars, and shouting out for fireflies or jugnus. These jugnus were her favorite flies, or whatever we call it. Whenever she used to spot one of them in the air, she used to shout out loud, and then get back to the conversation with further more excitement.

After an hour and half, I felt I knew her in and out, what she liked and what she didn't. What brand garments she wore, the perfume as well. Hey, no need to let your imagination run wild when I said "garments she wore." I am just talking about the Tee's and Denims; she didn't share the lingerie brands with me. Any ways, she was lost in her talk and me in her. Trust me, the girl whom I never looked at, or the one whom I thought was just a plain and ordinary girl, appeared to be the most beautiful on the face of earth. I started getting lost in her as she was trying to be herself. I was in a different world all together, where I could only see her and hear her. Final line that I heard from her that night was.

"You know what? When you told me we are going for a drive tomorrow? I was very happy. During the lecture today, I was singing a song. Aaj main khush hun and my professor caught me, when I was in a dream world which my friends told me," she admitted. "And he made me wait outside the class for the entire lecture," she continued.

As I said I was lost, my senses had given up on me, other than my heart which was beating in a slow rhythm may be to the ballroom beat.

Suddenly she looked at her watch. "Oh my God!" she said, "Nikhil it's 8.45 let's go."

I had heard her but there was no response given. She shook me and I came back from Wonderland as Alice was already back.

"What happened?" was what I said after what seemed an hour and a half. Ninety minutes of a dream ride, misplacing all the 4 senses which fell back into their places as she shook me.

"My hostel closes at 9," she requested showing me her wrist watch, "Let's go."

I saw her watch and then mine as well, in the discussion we had lost one more minute. I took my glasses, kept them at the counter and paid the bill.

Took my bike off the side stands and started it. She jumped on the pillion seat and we vroomed. We had to drive on the wrong side for another 100 meters as there was a circle to turn around.

"I hope we don't get late," she murmured sitting behind.

"No you won't." I said

To that she continued saying, "I hope I didn't bug you, you

were listening to me and I kept on talking."

She kept on rattling and apologizing for the next 7 minutes until we reached the campus. It was 0854 on the clock when I braked just in front of her hostel gate. Many students watched us together, a few eyebrows went up, but that didn't make any difference to us. She got down from the bike and looked at her watch, and I looked at her.

"We made it," I said seeing a relieved face.

"Ya, but you drive so fast" she complained as her eyes dropped out on the latter part of the sentence.

"You said you were getting late," to which she interrupted saying, "It's ok. I will go now. Thank you for the drive Nikhil, it was the best day of my life," she said.

My right hand went on to my heart and my head bowed down. I guessed she didn't even know that I was honored, and I was feeling much better than what she felt. I didn't say a word but I guess my eyes did the talking. I saw a shimmer in her eyes too.

"Ok, then good night," she said.

"Good night," I replied in a confused tone.

She turned around and began to walk towards her hostel gate which was around 15-20 meters. I was still standing there, thinking I would leave once she disappeared into the dark. As she entered the gate, she turned around and saw me standing there, in the same place with same expression, a mild smile on my face. For a split second she was there and then she went inside. I saw Pamela and a few of her friends entering, she saw me and threw me a smile, waving at the same time to which I didn't respond. I started my bike and came towards the library. Tonight nothing else mattered to me, I didn't bother about who was getting offended as long as Saloni and I were happy. I entered the library to find a few students browsing.

"Hi Reena, is everything alright."

"Perfectly fine Nikhil."

"You can leave for the day…" I paused, "Oh, for the night I mean" I said with a smile and winked. I had this bad habit of winking at everyone. She smiled, handed over the cash and the accounts and she left. Belgaum is a very safe place but it gets very quiet after 9 pm. I never wanted to take chances with my employees. When she left I sat at the cash counter, I was reminiscing over the evening as her voice echoed in my ears. Something got triggered in me and I went into Google, and downloaded the song Aaj main khush hun, tum hi bolo main khush hun kyun? I heard it, for some time on repeat before I went home.

1 KISS

Every other night I used to sleep like a baby, but that night I hardly slept. I was tossing and turning every minute that I tried to sleep. I might have got to sleep at 3.30 am and that too for 2 hours. I woke up when my granny was making tea in the kitchen. I went up to her and she was surprised to see me. And yes, this time I wasn't rubbing my eyes nor was I sleep walking and I didn't fall from the bed either, I was looking all fresh.

"How come you got up so early?" she asked when she saw me entering the kitchen.

"I did not sleep the whole night" I said as I rested myself on the kitchen counter.

"Why? What happened? Is everything alright?" she asked me all these questions as she put the gas stove on simmer and turned around.

"Nothing much, I am fine and yes everything is alright," I replied.

Meanwhile she poured tea for both of us still looking at me.

"Here you go, drink some tea and try getting some sleep before you go to work," she suggested.

"That's what I have been trying to do," I murmured.

"What?" Granny shouted, but in a concerned tone.

I did not answer; we took our tea and went into the dining area. She started telling me about how I was in my childhood. How I used to get up in the middle of the night shouting ghosts. How I used to faint during the showers, I guess I was allergic to water or may be liked to be dirty and messed up. Not only that but I showered my bed during the night as well. I mean as per my granny I used to pee in the bed while asleep. That was the day after many years when I sat with her and we spoke our heart out, even in those last 2 months since I was there, we had never had such a good discussion.

"You have been the naughtiest guy in our family!" she said.

While we were talking my aunt joined in when she heard us

talking and laughing loudly. We all sat there until I left to work.

I went to the library, the same old routine followed till 12, when Saloni walked in. I was in my cabin with a doctor, who had come in to enquire about a medical journal. She glanced at me through the glass door, smiled and went ahead. She logged in and sat in her favorite place.

"Please pay 1400/- hundred at the cash counter and you can avail the facility." I told the doctor who enrolled for the membership.

I walked out when I was done with the query, which was striking me as a wrong time for him to be there. The song "Animal" from Savage Garden was playing in the background. I slowly cued Saloni's favorite song to play and moved out from there. She had sunk into her chair and the monitor placed was a bit high. I believe she hadn't noticed me coming to the counter and doing the song stunt. Reena was wondering about my sneaking act.

"Whatttttt," said Reena slightly moving towards her right to avoid my touch. "Hey, I am not trying to touch you or something, ok?" my mind said.

She gave me a weird look which I ignored. When the song from Savage Garden got over and the next song began, I saw someone popping out of her seat in surprise. She was all smiles and her eyes were trying to locate something and it was me. I was hiding myself behind the pillar which connected the wall dividing the router room and the cash counter.

When she was unable to locate me for quite some time and the song was playing in the background, she came up to Reena. That's when I appeared in front of her sliding away from the pillar with a smile "smoking." Exactly as Jim Carrey does in the movie "The Mask." The only difference being, he had that green color on his face, and my face was painted red, the color of love.

Reena was busy at her work on the computer, she did not notice Saloni. Saloni came and gave me a smile, to which I reciprocated with a wink. She went back to her place where she was sitting, and I guess she logged out and came back. We both sat on the couch for some time after she paid her bill.

"Hey Nikhil, Thanksss a ton" she said with that killing smile and holding my hand slowly.

I didn't do much, smiled back at her, as usual lost in her smile and touch. I was a bit uncomfortable sitting hand in hand as it was my office, at the same time I never wanted to let her go as well.

Now whenever she used to come to the center, this song played no matter if I was there or not. Even Sachin and Reena learnt about this. My attitude towards everyone was the same, but my perception towards Saloni changed. I started liking her the way she was. I continued to be a sweet talker with everyone, flirting with other girls but the intentions vanished. I was getting absorbed in one girl. I was seen most of the times with Saloni and her friends. The walks in the college park became frequent; visits to the ice-cream parlor were regular. The whole of BPT (Bachelor in Physiotherapy) students knew it was more than a friendship. All the guys in the college loved this beautiful girl and she in turn was with me. Her mere presence made the world look so beautiful; her smile took all the worries away. "Is this, what first love is?" "Is this the first feeling for someone?" were all questions on my mind, which was controlled by my heart.

As there were no cell phones with us then, all we could do is to meet as much as we could from morning 9 to 9 in the night. After that I was managing my work and she was with her studies. Days passed and one day on a Saturday afternoon, when I was sitting in the library, the library assistant came and told me that there was a call for me on hold. I rushed in and took the call.

"Hello," I answered the call.

"Hi Nikhil how are you?" said a very familiar voice.

The librarian was sitting right in front of me. I faltered saying "I am fine."

"Hey it's me Saloni," she said as I paused for a while.

"Yes, Yes ma'am, how are you?" I asked her to avoid landing in trouble.

"Hey I am sorry to call you here, hope that doesn't go against you."

I wanted to say, you are getting me killed and I would be out of my job any moment, nothing else. But I said "Yes ma'am it will, it will," as I rolled my eyes towards the librarian and back after a small complimentary smile to him.

"Is there anyone next to you?" she asked.

"Yes, there is enough stock here, the big gun," I fumbled.

"Oh, ok then listen. My friends dragged me to this movie and I did not get a chance to see you, so I wanted to know if you want to join us."

"No ma'am, that won't be needed. It's fine being here."

"Ok then see you, bye take care. And yes I am sorry again."

"Ok, then see you soon, take care," I hung up.

To all this, the librarian was all eyes on me with his spectacles slid down, and I was sure his ears were all up like that of a sweet doggie. He continued looking at me pretending to write something. I was wondering if he was writing down the communication which I had over the last minute and analyzing what it was all about.

"Good afternoon Sir, how are you?" I greeted him.

He took off his spectacles, kept the pen aside and looking at me, he replied "Fine, waiting for tomorrow." I realized he was waiting for Sunday, so that he can take his wife out for a nice lunch and then may be rent a porn movie. And some act following it, he looked to me like a horny dude.

Any ways, what would a man in his early forties do in India? Working the whole day handling 2000 students was mad, on top of it, sitting here in the middle of so many hotties may have been killing him from within.

"Oh! Great, hardly few hours to go then! Hope you have a great weekend, Sir," I said and started to walk towards the door.

"Who was she?" he asked me apprehensively.

"Oh, the person on the phone, you mean?" I asked him, turning around. He just gave a nod.

"She is my colleague. She wanted to know if I needed anything here as she is coming next week" I rep-lied

"She has a nice voice," he smiled. "May be you can get her here when she comes to Belgaum," he added.

Then I knew he was surely a Chamdi like me, and tomorrow the deal was on - all the walls are going to get banged and the mattress is surely going to feel the pressure.

"Yes Sir, sure, I will," I concluded.

After stepping out of there, I was wondering how this Bond-kid found out the librarian's number. Then I realized that it was me, who had told her about my line of communication with my superiors. Never under-estimatewomen power and never give them your work secrets, they may play spoilsport.

I went back to my den in no time without any further thinking. In the evening after the movie, around 6.45 pm princess walked in. She was wearing a plain white shirt and light blue denim, her favorite combination.

She was accompanied by her friends Zainab and Priyanka. Zainab as usual cracking her PJ's and Priyanka giving high fives to her on every sentence she uttered. I was with a student and helping her out with the query she had with the login. She was a Punjabi girl, Paramjeet Kaur and you might have guessed it by now, she was beautiful. I was standing next to her. The query was solved and I was ready to leave.

"Why does this problem happen every time?" she asked me.

I looked at her for a while and said, "May be to give you an opportunity to call me."

"Very smart," she said and started laughing.

"Any ways, you have fun," I said and came towards the

counter.

I saw Saloni standing behind Sachin. I saw and smiled at her, a smile which continued from Paramjeet's cubicle. When I walked up to her, I saw the other 2 champions sitting there; they were discussing the dialogue of the film they had seen in a funny way. They looked like a pair of Abbas Mustan "sex changed" transgenders, and trust me the way Zainab used to laugh was crazy. She had a very cute laughter but sounded really funny, when she used to laugh one could see all the 32 or whatever number of teeth she had. The second one Priyanka was the extreme opposite, she laughed with her mouth closed, like a truck which is having trouble getting started, eheeeeeee, eheeeeee. May be like a malfunctioned skin toning belt, if you sat on the couch while she laughed, you would move, as you move when in a roller coaster ride.

"How was the film?" I asked Saloni.

"It was good," she replied.

I heard something in chorus, "It was funny and it was awesome."

"Only 3 of you went? You said 'friends' right?"

"They all went to the hostel, but Miss Saloni wanted to meet you so we came here," Zainab giggled.

"What was the name of the movie?" I inquired

"Lagaan" this time it was Priyanka who replied, while Zainab laughed again.

To avoid her shouting we both moved away from them, near the couch.

"What did you say? Lagaan, what kind of name is that?" I asked anxiously.

"It means a tax," Saloni said.

"Wow, how did you know?" I asked.

"Because we watched the movie!" the answer came from all the 3 in unison and laughter spread across the center.

I was surprised when I came to know that there was Aamir Khan in it. And to top it up, the cricket match sequence which happened to be the talk of the town. Man, hats off to Ashutosh Gowariker, he is truly the man of period cinema. As we were talking Zainab stood up and said.

"Nikhil, I need a favor from you."

"What is it that you want now?"

"I want you to download a song for me, please!" she ordered.

"Which one, tell me?" I asked.

She started singing the song and got up from the couch… Jisie dhundti hun main har kahin, wo pari wo hoor wo naazneen….. wo ladka hai kahan? And with the chorus wo ladka hai kahan, she imitated some weird step like a baby kangaroo trying to fly, and whenever she moved it was completely out of rhythm. I was embarrassed as there were some doctors walking in to the library, so I moved a few steps behind, but she continued without any hesitation and finally finished her performance.

"What's the name of the film?" I asked.

"It's Dil Chahta Hai" was the reply from all the 3 with a smile. They had a great coordination of saying something in harmony. Priyanka told me that even in this film Aamir Khan was there. I used to wonder at the titles of our Bollywood films. "Dil Chahta Hai, Kaho Na Pyaar Hai, Kuch Kuch Hota Hai" and so on.

Saloni added "Saif too."

I was unaware of these films' releases. I never got a chance to watch television at home; in fact, I was never home. Saloni ordered me that we should go to watch Dil Chahta Hai together.

I looked at her eyes and said, "Sure, do you want to go for a drive now?"

She smiled and nodded. Priyanka and Zainab took off to the hostel. I went to Sachin, told him that I will be back in some time and we both left. For

Sachin this became a routine, he used to manage it all by himself, almost every evening between 7 and 9.

We went to a restaurant off the national highway, to Hotel Ganesh. Every third place in Belgaum is named after Lord Ganesh, like the juice center as well. We sat there for some time with some snacks and a cup of tea. After an hour we drove around for some time and when we were returning back to the hostel, Saloni showed me a back way, a short cut, which the students used to take to commute to the hospital during their practical. It was a short cut and it was in the same campus. That place was completely in the dark, it had a small stadium in front, and the road which I followed to enter, was so narrow that it allowed only one car to pass by, with trees on either side which stood around fifteen to twenty feet tall. It was a dense area and there were no passers by at that time of the night. It had a basketball court and the stadium lights were on.

She asked me to stop the bike just before the basketball court.

"Why here?" I asked her.

"This is the way from where I will go to the hostel," she pointed out somewhere in the dark behind the tall grass, which was as tall as we were, I could not see the path as all I saw was trees and grass. So I kept quiet in order to avoid embarrassment. At a distance I could see some lights, so I thought it was not that unsafe for her to go to her hostel at that time. I stopped the bike, she got down.

"It's 8:30," she said looking at her watch and starting to look around.

I thought I could express what I felt for her now as this was the right moment. We had been together but never expressed what we felt for each other. I knew that she liked me through her friends.

I got down from the bike, put it on the side stand and leaned on to it. I was looking straight into her eyes and she was looking into mine.

"What?" she said with that sweet giggle, putting her hand right in front of my eyes and waving it right to left a few times.

It was a nice ambience, completely dark other than the light from the stadium around 50 meters away. I was thinking how to start and did not get the right word to begin with. As they say, even if you know that the other person loves you, it still happens to be difficult toexpress your feelings to them for the first time, whereas, in a one-night stand, you jump on to the other person like a hungry dog.

I got the courage and started with "You know…" She excitedly raised her hand towards me.

"Hey see, a jugnu!" she exclaimed. Her hand was over my right shoulder, pointing behind at the green fly.

I turned around in embarrassment and saw one. She continued showing me a few more, pointing at each of them as if they were like airplanes for small kids. I turned around after a while, but she was busy in admiring them and I was following her as usual. It was really nice to see her behaving like a kid; she was really a sweet child. Every time I looked at her, she was more stunningly beautiful for me. She came back to the world where I was waiting for her to finish. She looked at me as I held her hand.

"I am in love with you," I said as we stared at each other for a fraction of a second, and she told me that she loved me from the very first day she saw me.

"What a fool I am, I would have accepted you then. These many days have gone wasted," I said.

"Don't worry, I will make you make up for it," she said with that beautiful smile on her face. And leaned towards me again staring in my heart through my eyes and that's when we exchanged our first kiss. We kissed each other for a minute I guess, and then she hugged me tight.

"Thank you, thank you Saloni for coming into my life," I whispered.

"The pleasure is all mine, Sir!" she whispered back gripping me tight.

Life will never stop interrupting you in good times; it may be late in bad times though.

I saw a light falling on the tree in front of me, it was coming from behind,

Saloni too spotted it. We were proved wrong that no one comes here, so she turned around and leaned on the bike, and faced me pretending we are just talking. I faced the road so that whoever is coming cannot see her.

When the bike crossed us I saw my watch, it was 8: 50, but I did not tell her as she was busy watching where the bike was heading. I was keen on exchanging few more kisses.

We kissed again for some more time until she realized it was almost 9.

"Oh, It's late," she said letting go of her grip on me.

She looked at me and hugged me again, and coming closer to my ear she said "I don't want to go." I don't know if we call it whispering or a lighter version of it.

"I too feel the same," I said.

To that she replied with a sweet smile "If I don't go today, how can we meet tomorrow?" This was real filmy and I am sure she was all inspired from Bollywood.

She gave me a peck on my cheek and left. I stood there for some time till she disappeared and re-appeared again under the lights at a distance.

This became our routine. A tea at 7 at the Ganesh hotel, drive on the edges of the city and then back to the stadium, nice half an hour for kissing and home. There was one thing which she always complained about, and that was about my fast riding, which I always ignored.

1 MOVIE

As we started getting closer, everything started becoming nice and pretty. As our love was blooming Priyanka made an online friend. He was from Bombay and had some business in Goa and Belgaum. His name was Pinal, an average looking guy with an average height. In fact, he looked shorter than Priyanka. Might be, he was overshadowed when he accompanied her. Everything was average about him other than the money he had. He usedto wear spectacles which he always fiddled with, he was like a kid just as his girl-friend and Zainab were. They say two is a couple and three is a crowd, here two was trouble and three torture.

Priyanka, Zainab and Pinal all three rocked with their PJ's and pathetic sense of humor. Saloni and I, we hardly used to laugh on their jokes, as we never understood them. He was a Marwadi, but behaved otherwise unlike the people from their community. He used to spend lavishly, whenever we used to go out, me, Saloni, Priyanka and Pinal. Zainab used to stay away from us, as she never wanted to be an interruption other than on the college campus. God saved me; she had a little bit of common sense.

One Sunday we were having our dinner, Zainab was there too. The next week's mega release was Dil Chahta Hai. (Note: There is a problem with this information. Lagaan was a film that released several years after Dil Chahta Hai. Do you want to change the name of the film?) They all wanted to watch it, Pinal was in the mood to watch it first day first show. "Nikhil let's watch it first day first show," said Pinal. Priyanka was excited when she said, "We don't have lectures also on that day."

"I don't think the tickets would be available," Pinal added positioning his specs right, on his nose.

"No matter we will manage it somehow," said Priyanka as she exchanged looks with her sweetheart.

"I stay there, I will see if I can manage to get them," I said as I was staying very close to the theatre.

Zainab jumped in saying, "You have some friends here

right?"

"But the tickets should be available for him to get it," said Saloni.

The discussion was in full swing, and everyone was looking at us seeing all the 3D animation. We finally boiled down to buying the tickets in black by paying more if required.

I touched Manik for a favor, and he agreed to get me the tickets. He had some contact in the theatre. On Friday we went to the theatre at 2.15 for a 3 pm show, it was a completely packed house with a big 'House Full' board in place. I met Manik at the theater and introduced everyone to him. Zainab convinced him to join us for the movie and everyone agreed with the decision. He managed to get the tickets and we finally made it to the movie.

When the movie started and Aamir Khan was on screen, I realized why everyone was gazing at me. He had the same Goatee on his chin and the same spiky hair style as mine. Everyone must have thought I had imitated Aamir, but then I wanted to tell them that style is my copyright since a long time. The movie continued and as we all know it has been a cult in Indian cinema. All the songs were mind blowing, no comparison whatsoever.

Shankar Ehsaan Loy's music and Javed Akhtar's lyrics, awesome script and powerful characters made it a complete treat. Everyone had something to offer. The best part for me was to watch that film with Saloni and that too hand in hand. Most of the time, I was watching her and the expression she had on her face reacting to the different moods on the screen. I still remember, when the song "Jisey Dhundta hun main" played we were watching each other. I felt as if, we both would be on the screen anytime like Saif and Sonali Kulkarni.

Finally, when we stepped out, the thing that stuck in our memory was laughter and the character of Christine of course. Pinal, Priyanka, and Zainab took a rick, me and Saloni drove away on my bike and Manik went home.

Saloni wanted to visit my house but I declined, as I had already been out of the library for almost 4 to 5 hours. So I dropped Saloni to her hostel and went straight into the Library. Another month was just over recently, there were mails pouring in from all the departments congratulating me for another milestone. In the month of May, we touched a collection of a lakh of rupees.

Sachin told me that my Boss had called me twice. I went ahead and called him back.

"Hi, Kartik here," he said as he answered the phone.

"Good evening, Sir, Nikhil here."

"Hi Nikhil, how are you?"

"Absolutely fine, Sir, thank you," I replied.

"I had called you twice, but I believe you were busy?" he inquired.

"No, I was out for a movie. Some of the college students forced me to," I accepted.

To that he didn't say a word. He was convinced, moreover,

he believed in a people's person policy. He knew all the student and doctors were happy with me and the numbers spoke for themselves too.

"As long as the targets are achieved I have no problem what you do there," he informed me. I was relieved.

"You touched another high last month, great going, man!" he acknowledged.

"Thank you, Sir," I responded with a clear voice.

He said "Big Boss has some major plans for you, The center in Bangalore is not operating well and you may have to go there, train those guys for some time and get it on track."

When he told me that Big Boss had some plans for me, I could remember the scene when he opened his bag in the hotel and a separate compartment of antibiotics had made its presence felt. It brought a funny smile on my face, good thing he was not in front of me.

"Why not, Sir," I replied.

I never wanted to go anywhere else, away from Belgaum. As I was living in the moment and this moment was surely memorable.

1 CELEBRATION

It was July. Everything was rosy for me. My love had blossomed and my job was going very well. My salary had been hiked from 8K to 10K. There was some small occasional friction between me and Saloni, sometimes on the topic of my rash driving and sometimes either of us getting possessive. I happened to be a very positive man, however suddenly a drift towards negative thoughts started taking over. There were many fan followers for Saloni and her smile, and I was afraid of losing her. And on the other end, many girls wanted me too, which Saloni didn't like. So the friction started taking place from both the sides. Trust me, possessiveness and ego are the 2 biggest enemies of people in love.

On July 7th in the evening, Saloni, Zainab and Priyanka came with a cake in my cabin, the occasion being my birthday. We started the celebration, when, to my surprise the Chairman of the college walked in. As my cabin was the first one after the entrance he saw these girls inside my cabin. He must have been wondering what his college students were doing there in the cabin and particularly, when they were wearing their Lab coat, which meant it was during their college timings. I guessed he might have come to visit the library and walked in here as well. He didn't stay long, he went back immediately, looking into my cabin while returning back as well.

I didn't react, well, I mean with the girls, and seeing this Saloni got a bit upset. We distributed the cake to everyone, who was there in the library at the time. After that session, we all thought of having a bite and headed for dinner that these girls had thought of for a long time. Pinal was not there in town so it was only the four of us.

It was The Greens Restaurant, one of the most famous in Belgaum at that time. It happened to be far though, around 12 km; we went on and had a nice candlelight dinner. Guess! A candlelight dinner with your girlfriend and her friends. Wow, that was amazing.

We finished our dinner around at 8.15 and decided to go for a drive. Zainab and Priyanka went back to the hostel taking a rickshaw. We were hanging around in that area for some time and somehow the topic of Mr. Chairman surfaced. There was a short argument between Saloni and me; I knew it was my fault. She wanted to go back to the hostel as it was getting late. Anyways, we drove back to the college campus, but the way I drove was way too fast. When we reached the hostel, she got down immediately, trust me for almost 15 minutes, throughout the drive we had not spoken to each other. Not a single word and that aggression came through in my driving. She got down; she looked at me in anger, with her eyes almost moist.

"This is the way you drive," she complained.

"Why what happened"?

"What happened? After driving so fast, you are asking me what happened! Are you in your senses?" she burst at me

She was louder than her normal voice and definitely angry with me.

"It was just a bit faster than normal!" I replied with no regret on my face.

"I am sure, when I am not there you may be driving much faster than this," she added. "What if something happens to you? What if something happens to us?"

"Nothing will happen to us, I drive to the level where I can control," I said.

"Good for you, then drive yourself!" she said, and started to walk towards her gate.

I got pissed and I started the bike and accelerated it fast, but there was no response from her, she continued walking and never looked back. I drove down and came to the library, thinking what went wrong. I could not fix anything in my head. After a lot of thinking I realized, that the whole thing was my brainchild, my mistake. She tried to celebrate my birthday and I in return got mad at her. I drove fast which she did not like and expected her to understand.

There was only one way out to apologize for this. I went out and called at her hostel number, which I sometimes used to do. But you know what; her hostel line was much more famous and busy than the lines of Kaun Banega Crorepati. I would have at least got a chance to be with Mr. Bachchan on the hot seat, if I had put my time there. But this time I guess I was lucky I got through to the number in no time.

"Hello," said a woman, who was the warden.

"Hello, may I speak to Saloni from room number 55 please?" I requested.

She didn't say anything kept the receiver aside; I was saying hello, hello. No one was speaking and after few seconds I heard someone shouting, Saloni, room number 55, call for you. The same paging happened some 3, 4 times. I heard someone running down the stairs. In a few seconds Saloni picked up the receiver.

"Hello," said she.

"Hey Saloni, it's me. And listen I am sorry for what happened today," I apologized.

"Ok," was her reply.

"Hey don't take me wrong ya, please!" I requested.

"Alright," was what I got to hear.

"I love you," I said

She didn't say anything and hung up.

The whole day I felt as if it was just another 4th of July celebration, when America got independence, but everything disappeared like Saddam Hussain bombarding full throttle in the night.

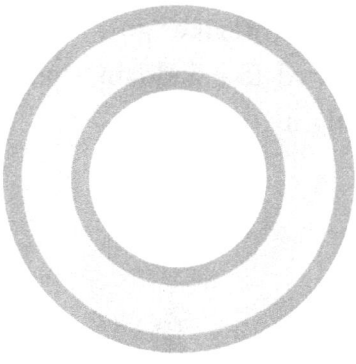

1 FIGHT

Last night had been bad for me, and I was sure it would have been the same for her as well. The next afternoon Zainab and Priyanka came to the library.

"Hey girls where is Saloni?" I inquired.

They looked at each other to decide who would go ahead and lie.

"She is attending a lecture," said Zainab avoiding eye contact.

"Are you sure?"

Yes, was their reply.

"Hey listen," I said, "I know she is upset with me since yesterday. Please tell her that I love her."

They looked at me, then went ahead and started browsing. One full day she did not come to meet me. The next day she came in the evening, and I didn't waste any time in taking her to the park. We sat there talking but she was upset.

"Hey! you know what?" I whispered.

"What?" she said.

"I have written a poem for you!"

She looked at me with no excitement and made a weird gesture by bending her head down. Any ways, I went ahead and recited what I had written.

Once I finished the poem, she looked at me and hugged me. Never thought it would be so rewarding, she gave me a peck on my cheek too.

"I am sorry, sweetheart," I said, taking her face very close to mine and looking straight into her eyes.

She smiled, hugged me again and said "I love you too"

Once everything simmered down, she went ahead and suggested something to me that I would have never thought of.

"You write so beautifully, you should continue writing more professionally," she said.

"Why? Do you wanna be upset with me all the time?"

She hit me right on my heart stabbing me to death with her soft fist. She smiled, "No I mean why don't you try writing professionally?" she suggested.

"Oh, yes that I can do, but you have to be my inspiration," I added kissing her on her forehead.

"I will surely inspire you for writing but not for rash driving."

So things were sorted out again this time as well. With me this had been happening for the last 2 months, when she used to get annoyed and I used to convince her. But yes, she had given me a good suggestion.

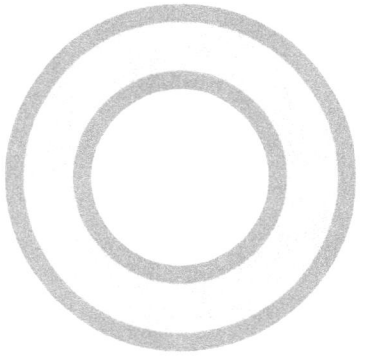

1 TRIP

I thought over what Saloni told me for over 2 weeks, and really started writing. I wrote anything and everything on nature, the general public and of course my love. During this period, Ruta suggested I meet a musician from Bombay, who was her Father's client. Her dad was a dentist too and she was gearing up to be one, I never knew that for breaking or manipulating teeth you get paid a bomb. And that's why so many students enrolled for Dental Surgery. It shouldn't be a surprise if we see some goons getting into this business of uprooting teeth legally. Any ways, I took a short trip to Bombay to meet him with all my poems and songs.

Trust me I wasn't a great writer then

but yes, I had love after all. Sounds like an old Hindi dialogue "Mere Paas Maa Hai."

There was a friend of mine staying in Vasai, so I decided to take a pit stop at his house. My friend was in one corner of Bombay and the musician was in the other. And for those who don't live in Mumbai, know that traveling a distance of a kilometer it takes an hour sometimes. Besides that, getting into the train during peak hours or shall I call it being pushed into the train and out is so effortless. All one has to do is to stand on the crowded platform, and in no time you will find yourself in a bunch of stinking commuters when the train arrives.

The thing was, I had no idea of all this before coming here. The next day, early in the morning we left for the station. It was 8.30 on the clock, when I reached the platform; there was no place to stand. And when we were getting down from the foot over-bridge, I saw a train leaving the platform where I could see people hanging out of the door, with one foot in the air and some sitting on the rooftop feeling the breeze in their hair. As it was all crowded my friend told me to keep my wallet in my front pocket. I was walking behind him like a small baby that follows his parents in the market place, with his head high looking at the new experience unfolding before his eyes. There came another train hurtling towards us. I could see from a distance that a few people were already there on the roof. "You come ahead," said my friend and pushed me in front of him. I kept on moving as he advised. The local stopped and we were pushed as mentioned earlier. I don't know what to call it, GETTING IN or FORCED IN. I was a fresh victim; I could see and feel somebody touching my bum, a few in the humping mode, and some hitting your face with their elbows and slapping and many more things. It all happened for a few seconds and then I found myself in the train as the train took off, my friend guided me to stand aside and made a place for me to breathe the not so good air inside. We went inside where the seating was organized. Oh actually it was not organized at all. 4 people sat in the place of three, the 4th one resting half his ass in the air. We went inside and stood in front of these 8 people sitting. It was a bad position to stand, with your butt facing a bunch of 4 and your front the other 4. After a few stations, we got a place to sit, and then in some time we reached the Mahalaxmi station.

"Take him to Altamount Road," my friend guided the cab driver.

"We will meet here in the evening," he told me.

I sat in the cab, and I realized the shirt which I wore was crushed like my vital parts at a point of time. "Oh shit" I said, "how would I go like this to meet him?"

The taxi man looked in the mirror and gave me a free piece of advice.

"Sir, don't worry, the person living in Bombay will never

feel bad about your dressing, unless he is from somewhere else, and this is how everyone round here is," he said.

The relief for me was that this guy was from Bombay, after a drive of 15 minutes from Mahalaxmi station we reached Altamount Road. It was 10:15, he had called me at 11am, so I waited downstairs, had a few cups of tea, and some breakfast as I had not eaten before leaving home.

I went in at 10:55. When I rang the door-bell, his servant opened the door. I was a mess; my face was full of sweat, shirt crushed. Mr. Shah came from inside, by then I had relaxed somewhat in an air-conditioned room. With two glasses of water already down the hatch.

"Yes, Nikhil, tell me" he said.

After looking at him I said, "Sir, I have been writing and wanted to see if I can try my hand professionally writing for you."

He looked at me, took off his glasses, looked again. "Show me what you have written," he asked.

I took out my favorite book gifted by my sweetheart. I started reciting, the ones he didn't like, he kept on saying next after a few lines, and the ones he liked, we went over them more than twice.

I don't know what it was, but he liked my thoughts and the way I put it on paper. However, he had a different suggestion altogether.

"This industry is not a very good industry Nikhil, it takes around 8-10 years for anyone to make it," he warned.

"And if you want to do it, you have to make sure that you have your regular bread and butter coming, and chase your dream simultaneously."

I looked at him for some time, but my mind was somewhere else. I knew I could write, it may have been a million dollar suggestion he had made, but for me it was peanuts. After a nice discussion I stood up shook hands with him, and left with a smile on my face. He didn't even imagine that this guy would be the next great lyricist. But I knew then that I am going to make it, no matter how hard it would be, right from the moment I stepped out from his residence.

I met my friend at the given address, where the taxi took me. I had the same fun back home on the local train with him. I went back to Belgaum on the same day as I had no leave and never wanted to stay away from my Love. After a week in Belgaum, Mr. Shah's words were still lingering in my mind. I just wanted to see how I could begin. I spoke to my Boss if I could get a transfer to Bombay. He had some other plans for me; He wanted me to handle the whole of Maharashtra as the Area Manager, after I set up the one in Bangalore. I was unable to make a decision, with so many things coming from all the corners of my small little mind. Would it be right to call it corners of my mind? I guess not, any ways, I am a bit bad with English myself. And I expect you to forgive me for that. Yes, so many things were shooting out of my brain like

Diwali fireworks, I was confused and had no idea. It was all unclear for me, I went ahead to share it with Saloni. She was super excited for me, planning to take it seriously and moving to Bombay.

"You should go, sweety," she suggested to me in no more than 2 seconds.

When someone's life is at stake it's so easy for people to say 'Just do it', no matter if the next step is hell. But she was the one who loved me, so I took it very positively. We went ahead and asked the other 2 members of this threesome gang. I got the same reaction; I thought it was just an echo of what Saloni said some time ago. If they were to race with MichaelSchumacher, I am sure these girls would have won all the races well ahead of him.

"Let's do it," I said.

I will go ahead and put in my papers right away; I decided and stood up from the bench in the park where we were sitting.

"Hey, chill!" said all the three in one voice as usual.

"First you should plan how you want to go ahead and then put in your papers accordingly," advised Saloni.

Did the same thing, went back to work for that day. I kept on analyzing for a few more days. "Yes I want to leave this job and go to Bombay", I told myself looking into the mirror. And guess what, the venue was the restroom of JNMC College. After a guy entered to pee that's when I realized, I was in a stinky place for planning my future, what a co-incidence, on one side of the walls it was written your future is in your hands, I was staring at those letters, when the other guy peeing saw what I was reading and then looked at me. He packed himself, washed his sins and left. I followed suit.

Straight from there I went in to write an email to my Boss, and clicked on send. It was 1st August, 01, within 15 minutes; the clerk from the college library came calling me.

"Nikhil there is a call for you."

I went and picked the call. "Hello, Nikhil here."

"Nikhil, my ass!" shouted my boss Mr. Kartikeyan. He didn't give me a single moment to speak. "What is this? What is this mail all about? What do you mean, you want to quit?"

"Sir, I…." he interrupted me again.

"Are you nuts to leave the job and go to Bombay" He whispered with a heavy voice. As if his jaw got stuck and he couldn't open his mouth with anger.

In a calm voice I said, "I know what I am doing Sir, and would appreciate your co-operation, and yes, I want to leave my job and go to Bombay."

"I am looking forward to seeing you as an area manager and you wanna quit now?" he yelled.

"Yes sir, I have made up my mind," I answered.

On hearing this, the call changed completely. "When do you want to leave?"

"A.S.A.P," I said.

"See, if you have already made up your mind and want to leave the job any way, let me request you one thing, give me some time until I find your replacement," he requested.

"I can surely do that for you, Sir. But I hope we find the replacement in a month's time."

"Let's see what Mr Rajnish has to say about this, good that you copied him on the mail as well."

Kartik was scared to death, as he was the India Head and the only center which was big in terms of investment and returns was Belgaum. Others were crawling and few had already been made to sleep like a tortoise facing the sky in a relaxed mode.

We finished the call, and in sometime Mr. Rajnish, my boss' boss mailed me, surprised.

We sorted out the issue, and it was decided that as soon as we got a replacement or 45 days whichever was earlier, I would be relieved from their services. For a moment it sounded like getting relieved from the armed forces after a battle of words.

1 FRIENDSHIP DAY

It was August 3rd, the first Sunday of August. Are you still guessing guys, I know the girls might know it already, it was Friendship Day. There was a trend in the physiotherapy course, that whoever had a birthday in a month would throw a party. And the bill would be shared among all the people having their birthday in that month. So August had 3 birthdays, Saloni, Zainab and Jacob. Jacob, the same guy from Pamela's group whom I had always thought was a guy who would be of no harm to a girl. But the reality was different, he was Pamela's best friend and had a crush on Saloni.

Ok, the story goes like this. As almost all the 1st year physiotherapy

117

students knew about what was cooking between me and Saloni, and most of them knew me, so I was also invited for the party. If explosives are there, there have to be fireworks, isn't it? I went into the party hall in Ramdev Hotel and was shocked to see it plain, with no decorations, nothing at all.

"Is this the place where you have hosted the party girls?" I asked, mystified, of Saloni and gang.

"Why what happened?" Zainab asked.

To which Saloni said, "We have all our parties here only." Sh-oo Sweet but dumb.

"But what do you do for parties? I mean, do you just come here, eat and go?"

"No, we play games, loads of games and music as well, see there are the

Speakers," Zainab pointed out in the corner.

When I saw the speakers, I thought my speakers in the library would be louder than these. Those were the old, hand-made speakers, with a big box and low volume, and if you increase the volume it would start sounding like some big huge man farting in a compact loo. I looked at the place and had a weird idea enter my mind.

We will decorate this place, I said and called the Manager, who was a friend of mine, as my boss used to stay in the same hotel and I happened to visit him. We had just 3 hours for the party to begin. We sent all the birthday people out. There were some students from their class who volunteered to help, and I had Priyanka and Pinal joining me in the show.

"What's your plan Nikhil," Priyanka asked.

I showed her my hand like the Congress election symbol, and touched my heart gesturing trust me. I guess Congress does the same thing. Pinal and Priyanka exchanged looks and followed me.

Things started, getting all the raw material, and getting the whole place decorated. There was one attraction for everyone, as it was me who was pioneering the project and my baby's birthday was to be celebrated, I made sure her name stood out.

It was show time, and all the guests started walking in. Everyone used to walk in, and stare at the wall where the names of the birthday members were written. I had used Styrofoam cuttings for the letters and pasted colored paper over it.

Saloni too walked in with Zainab. Both were neatly dressed, Saloni was wearing a black knee length skirt and a white top, and Zainab was wearing blue denims and a black tee. They walked in and came straight towards us, i.e. me, Priyanka and Pinal.

"Hey how do I look?" asked Saloni with excitement, and her

killer smile spread across her face.

"Superb, as usual," I said. To that Zainab asked us how she was looking.

Pinal and Priyanka said, "You both are looking smart and neat."

To which I added, "You look like the one making an advertisement of some talcum powder, look at your face, it's white." Trust me there was nothing so funny, as usual I was trying to bully her. And I succeeded.

She was embarrassed and started making faces, rounding her lips and lifting her nose, like the fish, which has that round mouth, looks as if it's desperate to kiss. Meanwhile, Saloni turned around and saw the names and started laughing. Saloni immediately moved 360 degrees, I guess she was trying to locate me and yes she was, I moved behind her trying to escape being caught. Finally she found me right behind her.

She smiled, "What is this, Nikhil?" she whispered.

I said "What? What do you mean by what is this?"

"I mean the names, why is mine in such big letters and colorful and others' small and plain."

"May be it's because I love you, and I was decorating that's why. And I guess no one loves them," I whispered back and winked.

Her name was in the limelight and it was something may be even a small kid could differentiate. She was half embarrassed any ways, Priyanka, Pinal were all giggles in one corner, Zainab was ok with it. The guests started flowing in and Pamela walked in too, stunningly dressed. It was like a hot piece of iron had been wrapped in a golden foil, which made the golden foil melt and sulk into her. Ooh, la laa!!! She turned around, looked at the wall of attraction and was shocked, as she was already angry with me and obviously jealous of Saloni. Meanwhile, all the guests were coming in, astonished and puzzled enough to look at the wall and then look at Saloni, and then finally scan me.

For some time I felt as if President Bush had handed over USA to the Iraqis and surrendered himself to Mr. Saddam Hussain for life.

Finally, we started the function; all the birthday members were called to center stage. They were briefed with something.

"Hey, what are they discussing?" whispered Pinal in my ears as we all saw the huddle on the stage.

"I believe they might be telling Saloni to pay more for stealing the show." I guessed it was nothing, other than the games and the proceeding of the evening. There was an announcement made and it was the first sequence of the evening. 'Passing the ball' they called it, but I never played it. I never believed in any social activities earlier and anyway I was doing this for love. My eyes were laid on her and hers on me; I saw her coming towards me again.

She came close to me and whispered, "Sit right opposite me!" it sounded as if she wanted me to kiss her in public.

I could barely hear anything, as there was so much noise in the background. Priyanka and Pinal thought we were just trying to get naughty, they were thinking on the same tangent as my dirty mind would have any ways. I held Saloni's hand as she turned around, to ask what she was trying to say. "Whattttt?" I growled.

She took her hand away and said again "Opposite me." I failed again to understand.

Most of the times it is difficult to understand girls, when they are speaking peacefully and this time it was complicated by such loud decibel levels around us. And especially when they make the sign language or whisper with their eyes all animated. Impossible!

She gestured again this time she was a bit far from me, but yes, I could read her lips this time. Those sweet lips, I could always understand what they say when they say nothing at all. She winked and went ahead.

Everyone started to arrange the chairs in a circle; it looked like self-service of not only food, but your seating arrangement and not a birthday party.

Everyone was grabbing a molded chair from one corner, where they were piled up. Everything said and done, I respect that person whoever invented or made the plastic moulded chairs, you can stack a whole pile of them in one corner. I guess once we cross a certain level of our population, may be, we would be sitting like that one day.

"Hey what's next? Are they already planning to have their dinner?" I asked Pinal. He went ahead and shrugged his shoulders, so we too joined the invitee to arrange the chairs.

The chairs were arranged in a circle, and everyone asked to sit randomly. Saloni took a chair, her eyes were looking at me, and getting bigger and bigger as she was gesturing me to come, and take a chair opposite hers. I was admiring her as anyone in love would do, it really didn't make a difference to me if someone was around or not. I was staring at her, like a kid gazes at the stars in the night, while his mother is trying to feed him, and who then gets a tight slap and is asked to sit down and eat. The same thing would have happened, if I wouldn't have reacted sooner, when I realized I saw Mr. Jacob, the birthday boy took the chair, the one which she wanted me to take; now her anger could be easily seen. And guess what I got to sit next to him; it was like 2 men loving one woman, sitting in front of her, for the verdict. It was just like the new reality shows on TV, where some stupid men get a chance to select from 10 to 15 beautiful girls. But, I already knew the girl was mine, I and Jacob exchanged a smile, and I was singing, The Girl Is Mine song in my mind. I saw Saloni making her move, shifting her chair abit, and positioning it in my direction, while I was sizing up my rival, about whom I had already been told by Saloni. Whenever he used to ask her out, she used to avoid him, with reasons like studies and her dear musketeers. But here it was going to be a different ball game and she knew it too. She was moving her chair so smartly, that no one noticed other than me. Some women are not only beautiful by their looks, but by the soft thing spread across their head called brains as well. The only thing is sometimes they use it at the right moment, and most of the times they don't. Finally after the long wait, and day's work of decoration, and running around and being watched by all the students the game began.

"Ok everyone, may I have your attention please" said the announcer. She was just another student, with a good voice, she was pretty as well. "We will be playing the first game for the evening, called passing the parcel." She added, "But there is a catch here, whoever has the balloon in his or her hands, when the music stops will have to choose a person. But yes, thatperson has to be sitting opposite to you. It can be a boy or a girl, it's your call. And the person in return will decide what he or she wants you to do. May be dance, act, sing or kiss as well." She stressed on the last word.

Suddenly I heard a huge applause, it was like the Filmfare Awards were being declared and it went to BPT 1st year students.

Any ways, the game began and music started. It was me, who had got the music from my Goan friends, whom I met in the college. It was almost trance and went well with the type of game we were playing. Just think, if a song like, Dhik Tanaa Dhik Tanaa was to be played from Hum Aapke Hai Sanam, oh! sorry Hum Aapke Hai Kaun film on this occasion. The music stopped for the first time, and it was Pamela holding the Balloon. Zainab was opposite to her, along with a few others so sportingly Pamela said, "I would want Zainab". It sounded like free beer and sex when she said it. Everyone started laughing at her, she was embarrassed, and Zainab was in her full, open Close-up style. Everyone calmed down, including Zainab who took some more time to control herself.

"I would want her to do pole dancing, she is best at it," Zainab clarified and laughed as usual.

Pamela was sporty; she was open for everything, I mean it anything, anywhere attitude girl. She stood up, looked around.

"But where is the pole?" she asked.

"Why don't you use Zainab as a pole, she is as good as a pole" Pinal suggested.

Zainab looked at him, her eyes widened and acute embarrassment on her face. I just smiled back at her, me, Saloni, Priyanka and Pinal, or let me say everyone in the party hall started laughing. She finally made her way to the center, while the Dj started playing the Santana song Maria. And trust me that was the best performance of the evening, it did not look like a pole dance any ways, Pamela was at her best, seducing Zainab to her level best. I thought Zainab might fall in love with Pamela and start dating her, you never know, she was any ways, stuck to her 2 girlfriends. The performance was over and we all gave them a standing ovation. This performance to us was just like having J.Lo and Britney perform together. I heard shouts of 'Once more!' from the crowd, but most of them were guys. Even I shouted once more without Saloni getting to see that I did. But unfortunately for all us, it was not performed again; we all wanted to see Pamela doing her moves. Any ways, we moved on with the game and it was fun to see people sing, dance or even kiss. After quite some time the balloon landed in Saloni's hands. The second birthday girl, after the first one had just sung her favorite song, Wo Ladka hai kaha in her scary voice, and I am sure that no one would want her after that. Everyone was looking at Saloni, she looked at everyone and then stopped at me, and Jacob's eyes were laid on her and mine too. In no time she said "Nikhil." So now it was official that I was her choice, Jacob's face was to be seen, he was laughing a moment ago with confidence and now he was quiet, shifting his looks around Pamela and everyone. I wanted to make it look grand which I had already planned, I looked at the (makeshift) DJ, who was a banquet manager, a very young guy. I had given him the CD of my favorite songs too.

"I would want her to dance," I said and paused, "with me."

She was smiling and really happy, as she had always wanted us to dance together, and we never got any opportunity.

Belgaum, as I said has no discs or pubs, so this was our chance, we both got up from our chairs, and made our way to the center; she was blushing and trust me, she looked beautiful with this new look on her face; I never saw her blushing before.

"Hey, thank you," she said as she came close to me, when we looked into each other's eyes.

I looked at the Dj and he played the song, I held her in my arms close to me and we started dancing. I was not that good in dancing, but not bad either and she was flawless. We danced for the entire song and no one dared or let's put it this way, no one bothered to disturb us by stopping the song, as the GIRL was mine and the DJ too.

Once the song was over, we realized that we danced for 6 minutes lost in each other. And to tell you, we were very close by the time the song was over, and when everyone started clapping for us, that is when we realized the distance between us and the audience.

"Hey, I am sorry," I said.

She gazed at me and kissed me on my cheeks and hugged me.

"I am honored," she whispered.

I don't remember what happened after that as I was numb.

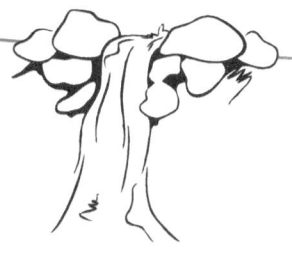

1 GOKAK

As the happiness was lingering in our minds post the party, Saloni wanted that to go on and she wanted to go out for a drive, a long drive. I could not say no to her. The place she wanted to go was Gokak, around 85 kms from Belgaum, and I had always heard that it is a very beautiful place. But I had no idea about the route. An idea popped into my head, I spoke to my cousin Ninad.

"Hey Ninad, how far do you think is Gokak?" I asked.

"About 2 hours' drive," Ninad said.

"Is it a nice road and a safe place if I take Saloni?" I inquired further.

"The road is good, but not that

great," he said, "and yes, it is safe."

"Oh that's great," I replied in a relaxed tone.

He was curious to know when I was going, as he was one of the wanderers in my family. Every other time I asked him a question, he tried to answer it hurriedly to ask me, if he could join me too, but my mind had more questions for him then than he had. He himself had many girl-friends, whom he used to take all around. He was like a walking talking recreation map; a cute looking guy aged 17 who was the hot property for all the Belgaum girls.

"So when are you planning to go brother?" he finally asked me once my quota of questions was over.

"May be on the 15th," I said.

After a bit of thinking and wondering, Ninad asked me, "Can I come with you guys?"

At first, I wanted to say no, but he was a sweetheart, so I agreed. After the decision was made, I advised him to bring his girl-friend for the trip. To which he answered, "Which one?"

What an idiot I am, whom am I asking this, and what type of a question is it any ways.

"The one who will come with you to Gokak," I said.

"Ahh, I will come alone," he shrugged.

I suggested to him, that if he had no problem then he could take Manik, if he wanted to join us.

Finally, the members decided on going were, me and Saloni, Ninad and Manik.

All were excited, and I thought, Saloni would have no issues, about my cousin and my friend coming. But I guess I was wrong, she didn't like it, though didn't show it to me.

"What an idiot this guy is?" she may have said to herself, when I told her the baggage we are going to carry.

Every woman thinks, she should be left alone with her boyfriend whenever they get to go out, especially if these chances come once in a blue moon.

Any ways, we were driving on 2 different vehicles.

On 15th I picked up Saloni from Triveni, her Hostel.

"Hey, look at you, looking cool!" she said when she saw me in a black, tight sleeveless T shirt, which had 2 weird logos on my chest. I don't know why I did that, as God never blessed me with a good complexion, which I can go ahead and tan. But yes, I had a nice toned build, and may be my intentions were to flex my biceps to everyone on the road while riding. I wore a cap and sun glasses, which were of 80 and 120 bucks respectively, bought from the fashion street of Pune, which was the extreme opposite of how Saloni dressed. Sometimes I used to wonder how come this girl loves me. I was an average guy, who didn't know much about brands.

"And you look beautiful as always," I said, as she was checking me out while I flexed my muscles.

Saloni was as usual wearing all the brands. She was wearing a lemon yellow T-shirt her favorite color, and off white jacket with a Capri and sneakers on.

Manik and Ninad were waiting for us near the Library temple at the exit gate.

They were on a TVS Fiero and we were on a Splendor.

"Hi Manik, Hi Ninad," said Saloni as we approached them, they said 'Hi' in return.

Manik and Ninad both were in T-shirts and track pants, they looked like trekkers. They were planning to do some swimming; even I wanted to be a part of that. We carried a pair of extra clothes, so that we could enjoy the water…

Gokak was known for its great water fall. We started the journey at 7 in the morning, and I did a wheelie. Ouh huh…. was my expression. Manik drove his bike behind us.

"Please do not drive fast, I warn you," warned Saloni.

"Just a good luck wheelie ya," I replied in macho style.

"I know," she replied.

We were on NH4, and then took a turn on to the country side road leading to Gokak. We were just 27 kms away in one hour, Manik and Ninad in front and we were following them. Saloni was holding me tight, and I could not even try to make her angry by driving fast. I was enjoying her arms wrapped around me as usual, so we continued our slow ride. Few kilometers away after another hour of driving, we stopped for breakfast at a small roadside hotel or whatever one can call it, it looked like a shack to me. It was made out of bamboo sticks, and had loads of grass growing out of the roof. It was not the only one like this, but all the hotels nearby were lined up in the same manner.

"So how was your drive till now?" Manik inquired, as we both got down from our bike next to them. Saloni stood right next to me, and as he asked us, she leaned her head onto my shoulder holding my hand. I was trying to be a bit naughty.

"It's been slow till now, may be let's have fun from here. Let's race, what say?" I replied.

Ninad was too excited about this. "Yes bro, why not, we have been driving really slow," he said.

Saloni moved away immediately and gave me a dreadful look. As a politician changes his party immediately after knowing, that the party he is in is going to lose. But here, I was in a win - win situation. We were 50 kms away from Belgaum, and I knew she won't give me that crap of 'Drop me here and I will take a rick or go myself.' But, I wanted that hug from her, so didn't exaggerate the situation.

"Hey, sweetheart, just kidding," I said.

"Don't ever do that," she said in a firm voice. It sounded like; she may say her favorite dialogue, anytime and wouldn't even mind taking a truck or a bus back home.

"Chill guys, let's have some breakfast. It's 9 30 in the morning," Manik said.

"Are you sure you will get something good here to eat" Saloni asked Manik.

"Of course, yes," he said looking at all of us, as if we all had visited this place before. And I am sure, he was not aware what he was saying, and he didn't understand what Saloni meant. She peeped into the kitchen which was completely open, right behind the delivery counter, which was square inshape. The waiters were in vests and loose trousers, which may have been washed in the 18th century, it was overall a shabby place. But I guess that's how it happens to be in small villages and I can't deny the aroma was too good.

"What do you have for breakfast?" Manik asked one of the waiters in Kannada. They were all standing and smiling at us, we were either aliens or some cartoon characters for them.

He replied in Kannada, which meant, Onion Bhajiyaa, Aaloo Vada, Idli, Puri Bhaaji.

We ordered few plates of Onion Bhajiya, Aaloo Vada and a plate of Idli. Saloni was not at all happy with the hygiene of the place. She was not against small joints, but cleanliness... I mean, I agree with her. She used to come with me to that small little Hotel Ganesh everyday, without a single complaint. But, here the situation was different and the tragedy was, we were all hungry, so I personally wiped the plates with some newspaper, which I requested from the manager, since tissues were out of the question. Finally, the dishes were served one by one. The aroma of those Bhajiya and Vada was so tempting, that even Saloni could not keep off from eating them. She too joined us in eating the so called un-hygienic but good tasting food. We paid a tip of rupees ten to the waiter as well, he had more blushing smiles on his face, poor guy didn't even know what tip was, he gave it to the manager. I had to fight with the manager and give it back to the waiter, where Manik's expertise in Kannada came into play.

It was 10.20, to be precise when we left the hotel; Gokak was another 30-35 kms away. We were on an adventure spree, nature and everything around supported us. Manik and Ninad were ahead of us, and I was purposely keeping a distance from them getting cozy behind. We had driven hardly for 20 more minutes and I had a flat wheel.

"Hey, what happened?" I said to myself looking at the weird behavior of my bike and braking.

"What happened sweetie?" said Saloni, coming out from her

dreams, she was still holding me tight. We both got down and saw the rear wheel was flat.

"Oh, no, how did this happen?" Saloni said with disappointment on her face.

I looked ahead on the straight road, there was not a single vehicle which could be seen, not even Manik and Ninad. They went ahead and we were left behind, they were in their own groove and returned only when they didn't find us behind them after a few kilometers. I had already dragged my bike for quite some distance by then.

"Hey what happened?" asked Manik.

"We were tired of riding this slow bike, so we thought of putting the engine off and walking instead. Save fuel you see," Saloni smiled.

Manik had got down from his bike, which Ninad was riding now.

"It's a flat wheel man," I said.

The scenery was beautiful, lush green all around, no houses for miles nor any construction sites and no passerby as well.

"Leave the bike," said Manik. "Ninad give that bike to them and come with me," he said and dragged the bike.

"But what do you wanna do?" Saloni asked.

"I will see if someone is interested in blowing air in it, or maybe I shall go back where it happened and reverse it, Déjà vu!" replied Manik, laughing.

"Funny, that's funny," Saloni said.

"We will look out for a tyre shop of course and get the puncture repaired. Meanwhile you guys be here somewhere or maybe, just follow us on the bike," advised Manik the great.

They took my bike and went looking out for a puncture repair shop. The whole scene of navigation and fun disappeared. We sat at a junction where Manik and Ninad took a diversion into a small village, after walking for almost 2 kms. We didn't even care about our friends who were doing our job, and we got lost in the beauty of nature. I took the bike 100 meters off the road and parked, as I thought it's a nice time to get some sweet kisses, after those hot bhajiyaas and vada. After an hour and ten minutes to be precise, these guys returned with the vehicle up and running. They decided to drive that bike themselves, by then I was fully charged with all those kisses. It was almost noon, and we were yet to reach our destination which we finally did at 12:35.

It was really superb when we reached Gokak. I and Saloni got into the small ponds which had flowing water and Ninad and Manik joined in as well. There was a huge crowd as it was Sunday. We had fun until 3.30, when we decided to pack up and return in case of any malfunctioning of any of our machines. If we had been all guys it was no problem at all, but I had my princess with me, and to protect her and to keep her safe was my motto. Though, I was the only one who put her in trouble most of the time.

That place is not only famous for the water falls, but for a sweet dish called Kardant. It's a nice mixture of dry fruits and jaggery. It comes in a block and weighs from 250 gms to a kilogram. When we went to a shop we found that in fact, every shop in that village was selling Kardant.

"Hey what is this?" Saloni asked me, looking at it.

"What is this, Sir?" I asked the man at the counter. He was a man with no smiles. He looked lost for a moment, looking at me from head to toe. It seemed as if I had committed a great sin asking him that.

"What is this? And how much is it for" I asked again both times in Hindi, but the man was still lost.

"Hey Manik, can you talk to him?" Saloni requested.

Manik and Ninad were in the mood for total fun. They were all drenched in water and had not changed into fresh clothes yet, they were still wearing their shorts and wet T-shirts.

Ninad and Manik stood right at the entrance of the shop, right behind me with their wet bodies. That is when I understood why the man was scanning me all the while.

When Saloni asked Manik to see what it was, they both entered the shop. The shopkeeper reacted to this in a funny way, his eyes stood out as if Ninad and Manik had got the Gokak falls into his store, which had been at his doorstep a minute ago.

"What is this?" Saloni asked him.

"It's Kardant," replied Ninad. "You should try this," he suggested pointing his finger at the sweet in the glass shelves while throwing a few drops of water on the old man.

Give them some to taste, he said in Kannada to the shop keeper. The man gave it to both of us, but still had no sign of a smile as he stared at Ninad. Ninad looked at him, and then looked at himself, and he realized what was wrong.

"Oh, sorry, I am sorry," he said again in Kannada to that man. "Just some water from your falls," he added, looking down at himself and raising his hand, thereby throwing a few more drops of water.

We loved the taste of that dish, and got it packed, bought some for everyone's family, and not to forget the 2 musketeers as well. Finally, we left and the time was 0430. That too happened after literally pulling out these 2 guys out of the water, which they kept on going back to. Overall it was fun, we returned back very smoothly, and we reached at 7. I droppedSaloni at her hostel, and that was the day when she told me for the first time, that she did not want to go to the hostel and wanted to be with me.

"I don't want to go to the hostel, take me with you, I want to be with you," she requested.

I looked at her, kissed her on her forehead. "No baby, you go to your hostel, we can't stay together now, and my granny and aunt will both bug you," I said with a smile.

She hit me on my heart, thumping it with her fist as usual. I declined her request and asked her to go to the hostel. If it was some other girl may be I would have not even thought once. But it was Saloni, I am sure it was because of the love for her, and the respect the feeling carries. I have seen many guys who don't get physical with the person whom they love, at least until they are married, I really like the culture which we Indians used to follow, which has gone for a toss now. The word which proceeds before love is lust nowadays. Has it ever happened with you guys, when your girl-friend asked you to take her home? I could clearly see in her eyes, what she wanted to say and what she was feeling at that moment. She was not wrong either; she just wanted to be in my arms. I kissed her on her forehead again and asked her to go to the hostel. Honestly somewhere deep down inside I felt the same too but had to control myself. She, like an obedient kid, walked back to the hostel, and as usual while entering the gate, turned around and looked at me with a smile and entered the gate.

1 BIRTHDAY

August 22nd 2001 was a wonderful day as it was Saloni's birthday. Though we already had celebrated it in the 1st week among friends, with me on the real day was different. But as Ganesh Chaturthi was on the same day, she wanted to go home, which she told me on the 19th, and that ruined my plans, exactly like that of a vehicle which is smashed under a hundred tonnes of weight, making it flat in one shot. That's how my heart felt that moment,100 tonnes of smacking weight.

She wanted to go home on the 20th which was a Friday, so I went to drop her at the railway station. I always made sure to give my princess a lotus whenever she was on her way home. A lotus, yes, that was her favorite flower, and I used to give her in style at the railway station.

"What a weird choice!" I used to say every time I brought that flower for her. How can someone like a lotus? Wow!

Sometimes, I used to be in full filmi style, going down on my knees and giving her the flower, I can't deny that. Girls like it that way; they expect their boyfriends to do it as the Bollywood stars do. We reached the station; she went to buy a ticket, I was following her 2 steps behind.

"Walk away if you want to, It's ok if you need to," I was singing the hit song while following her.

"So you won't be there on your birthday haan?" I asked as she joined the ticket queue and I stopped next to her.

"No baby, I don't think so." She replied sadly holding my hand.

"I had made so many plans for you," I paused "Any ways; we will do it when you are back."

She smiled, "Of course, yes."

Now it was her turn at the ticket window.

"One, Miraj please!!!."

She had this habit of traveling in a general compartment, which I always argued with her about, she never carried change with her, and she used to fight with the ticket vendor for 2 rupees, for more than 2 minutes. Most of the times I used to run behind the auto rickshaw guys to beg for change. Change is constant but change is a big problem. I used to look like the newspaper salesmen who sell papers at traffic signals, running around here and there.

Finally I managed to get the change of 10 rupees - from a beggar this time. He asked for his commission of a rupee which I gave him. The beggars make good money nowadays, they make more than an MNC employee with a degree.

"There was no need for creating a scene for 2 rupees," I complained to Saloni.

She looked at me, smiled and didn't say a word. We went to the platform.

We were 25 minutes before schedule as always, but had to waste 8 minutes in breaking that 10 rupee note. I gave her the flower when she sat on the bench.

"Here you go," I said, enacting a super hero.

"Wow, that's so pretty!" she jumped. "Thank you, sweetie," she said and checked to see if someone was watching and kissed me on the cheek.

"So what are you planning for decorating Ganapati?" she asked still admiring the lotus in her hand.

"Oh, me, haven't thought that far yet," I shrugged.

"What? It's day after and you have no plans for Him, he is your favorite God, right?" she was baffled.

How could I tell her that, I had been busy planning for her birthday instead.

"I have 2 more days" I said.

"2 more days, my bum, just tomorrow," she replied as she counted on her fingers, which was not necessary.

"I have tonight as well," I said winking at her.

This is the way we went on talking and the train came on time, when you wait for hours for the train to come it gets delayed, and when you don't mind it being late there it comes bang on time. It was 06:30 in the evening; I went in the train to find a place for her, it was packed, however we managed to get one seat.

She kept her hand bag on the seat.

"Can you please keep this seat for me, I am keeping my bag here," she told the lady who had occupied the window seat.

"Yes, why not?" said the lady.

We went ahead and stood for some time at the door, on the other side of the platform as passengers were still getting in.

"You take care of yourself and don't drive fast," she warned stressing on the later part.

"I will, I will. In fact, you take care of yourself and have fun on your birthday."

We heard the train saying, get lost, by its honking "Pom Pommmmm."

There were some people standing at the other door, so I kissed my baby on her forehead and got down.

"Please book a ticket in 1st class next time!" I shouted as the train left.

The train left and all my plans were run over by it. I went to the center, in which I hardly used to put my heart nowadays, which was just a month away from me being out of it completely. The business did not change, but the people, I mean the students there, were not happy with my idea of leaving. Other than a few like Jacob, who were waiting to celebrate their

Independence. I was sure that Jacob would be the happiest man, once I left and also all those who loved Saloni.

I left early to plan the Ganpati decoration, I went straight to my cousin's, where everyone was gathered.

"Let's make it different this time," Ninad said, as we began discussions once everyone came in.

"What do mean by different, please elaborate," said Sagar.

Sagar was fully under the influence of alcohol, and had the

ONE LOVE

fragrance of it following him all over the place. He had just passed out of college and managed his father's transportation and holding business. Every night, that is, post 7, he needed half a bottle of whisky to keep him running for the next day and for a good night's sleep.

"I mean every time we decorate it with a Pandal, and get loads of fireworks, let's not do that this time," Ninad replied.

"Then what should we do?" Sagar's younger brother Vaibhav asked.

"This time we will bring fruits and only fruits, and arrange it in front of the idol," Sagar said.

"That's an awesome idea but why not fireworks?" I asked him.

"Because every time we bring too many crackers, and it's not good," Sagar added. He continued, "I have seen this doggie which happens to be scared when any cracker is set off. There must be so many dogs around who are scared. Let's spare them this time," he said.

"Besides the pollution," Vaibhav added.

Vaibhav was Sagar's younger brother, and a very good cricketer. He was the extreme opposite of his big brother. He never touched alcohol, and women were a no-no for him. If everyone happened to be like him, the population would have been under control and I guess there would have been no rape cases around, either.

Wow! I was happy my cousins who are younger to me, were thinking wisely, unlike me who was lost, who didn't know what was happening with him.

Anyway, the plan was liked and approved by everyone.

"So who is going to bring the stuff?" I asked them.

"Me and Vaibhav can go and get it all," Ninad volunteered.

"I will be home at around 9 pm tomorrow, and then we can do the lighting and the rest of the stuff," I said.

The next day everything went according to plan, we decorated the house and the place where we used to keep the idol of Ganpati. The only thing that remained was the fruits to be arranged, which we decided to do early in the morning just before bringing the idol. The next day, we got up and got everything organized and went for the procession, everyone happened to be home that day. All my aunts and my cousins were there; my mom and sister had also come, dad could not join as he had some work in Pune, and I took a day off.

"He is looking stunning," said my sister looking at the idol after all the Pooja and formalities were over.

"He has always been stunning," I replied without looking at her.

"I know, I know," she said.

My mom said, "He already had a pot belly and these guys have piled up fruits in front of him. Why?" All elderly oldies started laughing at this.

Vaibhav jumped from one corner and said "It's for us so that we can put on weight and look like him," he laughed.

It was a perfect family function; everyone was in a mood for celebration, reminiscing, making fun of one another, and everyone occupied a seat wherever possible. Some were sitting on the diwan, some sat on the floor, while we kids stood watching all the entertainment.

I just loved that day and for a moment, I forgot it was my sweetheart's birthday, whom I was supposed to call and wish. As it was lunch time and everyone was getting ready for the 8 course menu, lots of vegetables, poran poli, modaks and what not, suddenly the phone rang.

Vaibhav went ahead and picked it up.

"Hello," Vaibhav asked.

"Hi, may I speak to Nikhil please?" said a female voice on the other side.

Vaibhav realized it was Saloni, he came slowly to me, "It's your gadbad," he whispered, Gadbad or trouble was a nickname we had given for girlfriend or any girl. And no one knew about her, other than my cousins and my sister of course.

I went immediately to the phone, and said "Hello,"

"Hey sweety, how are you?" said my love.

"Hey, I am fine, how are you? Wish you many happy returns of the day!"

"I am fine, thank you," she said.

"So how is your birthday going?"

"How would it go without you? I am waiting for you," she said mimicking in a child's voice. One can never be sure of girls, I mean, I always thought I had the devil inside. But here was the big mom of the devil.

"What do you mean waiting for you?" I inquired.

"I thought of celebrating my birthday with you."

"What are you saying? You back?" I asked her with all element of surprise and excitement.

"Yes I am, in fact, I went to the library, and I didn't find you so thought of calling you. It's good that you have a phone at home."

"Ok, listen I will be there in 20 minutes," I said.

"Drive slowly, don't rush," she suggested.

I got excited and left without my food, my sister wanted to join me, but somehow I managed to convince her, that I will introduce Saloni to her next time.

I went, full of happiness and when I reached, I saw Saloni sitting on the couch waiting for me. "Happy birthday, beautiful!" I said giving her a bunch of lotuses with one red rose in it, which I had managed to pick up in those 20 minutes on my way.

"Thank you so much, they are so beautiful," she said with all excitement.

"You had your lunch?" she asked.

"No, not yet. I wanted to have it with you."

"Ok, let's go then," she said

I took her to a specialty restaurant, where we had some nice Chinese.

Unfortunately we had to order veg. as it was Ganesh Chaturthi.

"What do you want to have?" she asked.

"Everything looks complicated and same for me," I said.

Trust me, for a person who eats non-vegetarian food most of the time it is difficult to order something vegetarian. It's like being given a choice of 20 Miss Sri Lankas to choose from, in which everyone looks the same and none popular to us at all.

"I know, but we have to eat something, right?" she said.

"I know," I said. I called the waiter for his special assistance on the menu.

"What would you suggest we have for lunch, what's your pick?" I asked him.

He was just another tambi of small joints in a big hotel, the only difference was, he was wearing a nice clean dress with a bow and yes he could manage to speak some English. He rattled off some of the dishes which were going over our heads like bouncers. Saloni tried to interrupt him; he was still going on with the menu list.

"Can we have 2 hot and clear soups, and one, mushroom fried rice please?" she said.

The dishes to me sounded good, just like Jai Ho from Slumdog Millionaire sounded to the Americans. We somehow managed to eat all that we ordered, and it was not bad at all. I burped few times as well. We stepped out after giving tambi a tip of 20 rupees and some change.

"Where are we heading?" she asked me when we reached my bike.

Surprise.....

After lunch we headed for a Ganesh Temple which is very famous in Belgaum, I wanted her to be there on this occasion.

When we reached the temple, I saw a long queue and people with garlands, coconuts, sweets. Man! Human beings will never stop bribing, and God won't be an exception for them, and that's why we Indians are left behind.

After looking at everyone standing with something or the other, I too went ahead and got some flowers.

"Wow, look at the temple!" she said.

It was fully decorated, with garlands all over, and the fragrance of different flowers was spread across the premises.

"It looks beautiful," I said breathing in slowly.

"You might have to go home as well, right?" she asked in a sad voice.

"Yes, but I will be with you until evening, if you don't have some other plans," I said.

"No plans. How are Mom and Mili?" she inquired. My younger sister's name is Mili.

"They are good, in fact Mili wanted to meet you, I told her tomorrow."

"Oh, that's so sweet, you should have brought her along with you," she said.

I ignored her. The time passed by and we entered the temple

right in front of the idol. Prayed together, all I prayed was for her long life and for her to be mine till the last breath. I genuinely prayed for her to be with me all my life as that was the only thing I wanted then. I looked into the eyes of Ganesh's idol, and there I got a confirmation that my prayer has been honored. Moreover, I too had bribed him with some flowers.

"Wow, yes!" I said.

Everyone next to us looked at me and Saloni almost broke few of my ribs when she hit me with her elbow gesturing what's happening. I nodded my head, saying nothing. Sometimes you have a connect with God may be due to your honesty or whatever and things do come true. Your prayers are answered but it has weird ways of coming real for us. We left the temple and reached our final destination Triveni hostel. There was one mistake which I had done, though. I was supposed to do the Ganpati puja in the evening at home which

I had forgotten. I saw the time was already 6 when we left the temple.

"Oh, shit it's 6, I am late!" I fumbled.

"What happened?"

"I was supposed to be home by 6 for the pooja"

"Oh!"

"Sit, sit, sit, let's go. I will drop you and then go home," I rushed.

While returning back I drove way too fast maneuvering on the high way.

The temple was on the outskirts of the city.

"Hey, drive slowly!" she shouted from behind me on the pillion.

I still continued driving fast. She continued telling me which I ignored till I reached the hostel. She got down immediately and started walking. I held her hand.

"Hey, what happened?" I asked. She stopped and turned around. I could see her moist eyes.

"Hey baby, what happened?" I asked her again.

"What happened? You drive your bike like crazy and ask me what happened?" she cried.

"But I had to go, you know it, I didn't do it purposely!" I tried to convince her.

She was not in the mood to listen to me and the blessing of God which I had got a few minutes ago started to wither.

"This is how you drive every day, every time. It's my birthday today and you drove so fast. What if something would have happened to us, to me?" she shouted.

"Hey come on," I said, "I am sorry. I didn't do it on purpose, Moreover, I have stopped driving so fast you know it."

"Good for you!" was the response.

That pissed me off. She was not able to understand the situation I was in and was throwing attitude at me. I am not John Abraham, that's a different story. But how could a boy take all this crap when he is just trying to make his girlfriend's birthday a memorable one?

"Ok, so this is what you have to say?" I asked.

She didn't utter a single word. I was still holding her hand. She looked at me with those eyes filled with tears and anger. She looked awfully bad in that look.

Moreover, you can get kicked right in the imperative places anytime, the only thing which can save you is the position I was in. I was on my bike, so I was safe and she didn't do anything like that.

"You are hurting me," she said.

I let her hand go. But she still continued to be there staring at me.

"I am sorry I won't drive fast again."

She didn't say a word but turned around and left. I was waiting for her to look back once she entered the gate but she didn't. If you happen to be strict to girls they bow down.

ONE LOVE

As soon as you say sorry, they take you for granted. I waited for some more time but in vain. It's very true only thing constant is change. You may never know what's going to change when. An hour ago I was praying for us to be together and in less than ten minutes this was the case. One thing I always have believed is that whatever happens to you, happens for the good.

1 REPLACEMENT

After that incident, she didn't meet me for 2 weeks. Zainab and Priyanka were also not co-operating with me. Moreover, my company had found a replacement that I had to train. And guess what, they, my company wanted him to learn the way I handled all the students. They were encouraging him to learn flirting indirectly. Everyone can't be Sachin Tendulkar.

"So Nikhil why are all the Bosses impressed with you?" asked my replacement. His name was Vinay, he was from Hyderabad.

"I really don't know, Vinay, if they are impressed, they would be the right people to tell you why," I replied.

"Ah ha…that's nice," he said.

My last date was confirmed as 30th September, 2001. I was at least happy that I would be out of this job. However, there was something killing me from within. We were already in the second week of September with no sign of Saloni meeting me. As usual, Zainab and Priyanka came to the library one evening.

"Hey girls how are you?" I asked, making them sit on the couch.

"Hi there, we are fine. And you?" said Priyanka as she parked herself on the couch to breathe free.

"It's good, not bad. In fact, not that good," I replied.

They could see in my face that I was not happy at all. And I am sure they knew what was happening with Saloni. However, they decided not to tell me anything.

"How is Saloni?"

"She has gone to her town," said Zainab looking at her watch.

"When is she coming back? She is mad at me, isn't she?"

"I don't know," she replied as she stood up, "may be in a week's time. Even Priyanka is leaving for Ahmedabad for a week. I wanted to go, but I won't as I have to complete some practicals."

"My last day is 30th September," I told them.

"Have you found any job, and where are you moving?" asked Zainab.

"I don't know, I haven't found any job yet. I may be moving to Pune for sometime."

"But you wanted to go to Bombay right?" asked Priyanka.

They were as surprised as I was. I didn't know what I was doing.

"Let's see, I don't know," I said.

When things are supposed to be bad, they will be, and will even get worse if needed. One day after having my lunch, I was returning to work, it was around 5. I was in my own world with so many things happening inside.

There was a car in which some guys were playing around on the road, they were cutting lanes (that road in Belgaum had only 2 lanes though), going fast and suddenly slowing down and braking. Which disturbed me a lot, so I overtook them peeping into the car, as they were driving like mad.

They started racing me and overtook me from the left. The driver was like Schumacher in the making. He showed his middle finger and drove past me. That finger can piss anybody off and of course, people like me who were pissed already. If he was trying to be Schumacher, I was not less than Valentino Rossi. I drove as fast as I can, maneuvering the traffic. Mine was a 100 cc bike, and he had a small car which would be at least 1100 cc, but yes, he had a car. I gave him a tough fight on the busy lanes as it was easier for me to take my bike out from wherever I wanted unlike him. Finally, on a straight road which had a left turn towards the college he came from behind and rammed me from my right side.

"Oh, fuck," I said as I fell down and went skidding for around 20 feet. He sped after that, he didn't stop. Anyways, who would want to do that after ramming into someone, where the possibilities were fatal.

"Ahhh!" I howled as I tried to gather some energy and got up.

I suffered minor bruises on my right elbow and forearm. My bike was scraped from one side. It was almost looking like a black and white with the indicator hanging like balls bouncing up and down. If Hero Honda had have seen it, they may have used this color combination for the next lot of bikes. Thank God nothing major happened to me, and I thought I was lucky to escape that accident. I wanted to chase and beat the hell out of them, but my bike didn't start as I was helpless.

The cop on duty out there helped me with some water to clean the wound.

"Are you alright?" he asked as he saw me lifting the bike and trying to start it, which it didn't, so he made me sit on the side of the road. Some guys who were passing by moved the bike to one side.

"Are you hurt? Are you ok?" asked those guys seeing anger in my eyes, simultaneously putting some water on my bruises.

"Am I MJ, who will start his moon walk and sing I am BAD; I am BAD? Of course I am hurt, damn it, can't you see the blood running out of my body and painting the road red and besides my bike's been fucked to the core. You guys ask me, am I hurt. However, that's the typical question all around the world anyone would ask, sympathizing."

I didn't say any of this out loud, just looked at them and kept quiet.

I gave the number of the car to the cop, for him to file a complaint against them.

I realized things have started going against me.

But then every bad thing has a good thing happening and a good thing has its bad effects. Two days later Saloni finally came to meet me, in the library. However, that was a wrong time award, trust me. It was as bad as an 80 year old man being given a Viagra. She came inside the library and saw me in my cabin. I was explaining to my replacement the backup plans and the people to co-ordinate in case of the line going down or any connection - related issues cropping up.

"So that's how you deal with it," I concluded, as most of the wrong times the RIGHT thing happens.

"Great, so BSNL office would be the place I may have to visit a couple of times," he paraphrased.

"Yes, I will introduce you to them tomorrow. Make sure you maintain a nice rapport with them."

"Sure."

"You be with Sachin, I will see you in some time," I said and left the cabin, he followed me and went to Sachin.

Saloni was sitting on the couch, she was surprised to see me in a formal shirt, that too in full sleeves.

"Hi, how are you?"

"I am fine, thank you, was busy with loads of stuff. Besides I went home for a week," she replied.

"Hey, you're looking good, since when did you start wearing shirts?" she asked.

"Thank you, sometimes I do"

"And how are you?"

"I am doing pretty good, just started the handover. My last date is 30th of this month."

We were very formal, it looked like 2 strangers who have

been made to walk for thousands of kilometers crossing the desert and finally meeting when all energy has been exhausted. To break the ice, I said, "Let's take a walk."

I didn't know that I was digging my own grave, we stepped out of the library. We started walking towards the park beside the temple, we went and sat on the bench.

"So are Mom and sister still here or did they go back?" she inquired.

"they are fine; they left already," I said.

"Oh, ok. Hope the Ganpati and all was good?"

"Yes, it was. Besides this handing over, everything has been good so far."

I held her hand and said, "I am sorry. I know I acted dumb. I promise I won't drive fast."

She looked at me and in a very low voice said "Liar. You always say that."

"I mean it this time," I said.

She had a way of saying LIAR, which I loved to hear from her. In fact, one day I wrote a poem on it as well.

After a while, we started walking back towards the library, it was 6 pm. The sun was still up but getting dimmer as an old man fading away.

"I will go now," she said.

I thought I had met her after such a long time.

"If it's ok, can I walk with you until the hostel?" I asked

"Yeah, ok," she replied

We started walking, passing the parking lot. She spotted something and stopped.

"Hey that's your bike right?"

I fumbled, as the bike was not done yet. It still had those hanging indicators which indicated that I am going to be hung like that. The scratches were yet to be re-painted, which was a sure sign of my heart being torn apart.

"Oh, yes. That's mine."

She went closer to it.

"What happened, what is all this?" she asked me.

I didn't say anything, which worsened the situation. I knew it has gone beyond my imagination. It took me three weeks to follow her up to meet me and now this is what came up. When your luck is not in your favor, don't worry, even a small pebble can hit you there and kill you.

"You met up with an accident didn't you? See this is what you do all the time, don't care about yourself and anyone."

I was quiet, listening to her so that the situation did not go out of hand.

She came close to me held both my arms around my biceps' and shook me.

"Why do you do this Nikhil?" she realized there was something wrapped around my right elbow. She started rolling up the sleeve. Which I tried to stop, as it was a public place, and it was not good for either of us.

Finally, she managed to see it.

"Hey it's nothing, just a minor bruise," I said after breaking my long silence.

She looked at my bike and then at me, I believe she was comparing the wounds we both suffered.

"It's a minor bruise you say."

"Yes, it's minor. Don't exaggerate. Moreover, It was not my fault, someone came from behind and bumped against me," I told her.

"Why are you lying? I know how you drive!" she said.

A bad man for once is always bad, your family and friends will curse you for driving fast, and if you meet up with an accident, it is always your fault no matter who is wrong. That pissed me off.

"If you know everything ahead of time, and you know that I am deceitful, cut the crap," I said.

"Yes, you are right. Let's cut the crap. I am fed up of all your allegations and these stupid acts!" she blasted.

"Yes, I know. Same here. Let's part ways then, why compromise?" I gave her back."

When we are angry, we don't know what to do and always do what is not to be done. And that's what happened.

There was nothing left, she just went away without even speaking further. I knew I was wrong, but she was not right either.

That was the last day we saw each other. The topic on which we fought and parted ways was not a big one, but we made it big. I agreed with her that I used to stop her from talking to guys it was not because she would start liking them, but she was way too innocent, and I never wanted her to be taken for granted. She used to stop me from driving fast and this was not because she was scared of dying, but because she cared for me. So we both cared for each other but had a weird way of expressing it.

Anyways, she left towards her hostel, and I went back to the library. Days passed by, we came close to the month end. Before I could go, I got another blow. Few of the students came to me who used to like Saloni, and she hadn't given them any importance.

"Hey Nikhil, how are you?" they asked in unison with a smile as if they just killed all the British which ruled India for ages.

"I am fine guys, how are you?"

These guys were like a tobacco factory, chewing their death, spitting out their lives all over, man that was pathetic. Imagine these guys wasting their parent's money for nothing.

"We heard that it's your last day today?" asked one of them.

"Yes, that's right." I replied.

"So where are you headed?" asked another guy blowing the tobacco juice out of his mouth on to the small plants on the road side.

"Moving to Bombay," I replied.

"Oh, that sounds great," he said. "Did you break off with your girlfriend?" he added.

"What do you have to do with that?" I burst out.

"Nothing, just saw her with someone else, so thought of asking you. Any ways, take care man."

They all left, leaving a whole load of questions in my head. I never thought I would have to go through so many things. Shifting gears from work, which was heaven, moving to

Bombay which I don't know what it would be, hell is what some would call it, and besides everything, this thing of love that had stung me. I looked up at the sky, talking to God.

"Why is this happening to me, why me God?" Exactly like Salman does in Hum Dil De Chukey Sanam.

There was no answer so…I thought of finding it myself.

At around 9.30 that night I went to a phone booth and dialed the hotline number of Triveni. After trying it for around 17 minutes to be precise I got through to the number. Every time I dialed this number I thought of being a millionaire and dialing the KBC number instead.

"Hello," said a pretty voice.

Wow, I wondered for a moment. I guess they have got some young wardens in the hostel. However the case was different. The phone had been picked up by another student who happened to be there.

"Can I talk to Saloni, from room number 55 please?" I said.

"Yes, sure," she said and called out the room number loudly. I had to take the receiver a kilometer away from my ear to avoid her shout tearing apart my ear drums. I guessed she kept the receiver, and then I heard another shout 'Call for Saloni. Room number 55, there is a call for you!' The same voice from a distance, this time it was better. I waited for some time and heard someone coming to the phone.

"Hello?"

"Hey sweetheart it's me," I said. There was a slight pause for some seconds.

"Oh, hi," she said with a clear voice.

"How are you?" It was what I thought of starting with.

"I am fine, and you?" she asked.

"Doing good. In fact, today was my last day in the library."

"Oh, ok," she paused for a while again. "And what else?" she continued.

Listening to this conversation, I felt strange and felt she was rude.

"Are you still bugged with me?" I asked.

"Bugged, for what? I thought it was over," she said.

That ripped off my heart, which was trying to be soft and my blood vessels started pumping to explode towards the mouth piece of the phone. And there was confusion in my brain as well. I knew that moment, there would be a crash landing.

"What did you say? It's over! Is that what you call love?"

She didn't say a single word but was listening to me.

"The entire thing we shared is over? I agree that I have been

169

wrong sometimes, that doesn't mean you were always right," I said.

"Listen Nikhil, I am in no mood to listen to this. I have heard this and been through it."

"What? I am going through hell, and you say you are not in a mood to listen to me. How mean can you be? Listen, if that's how it is, let's cut the crap. I don't want someone who doesn't want me. You take care."

She heard this and hung up the phone....

That was the end of the story. I stepped out of the booth full of sweat, my heart beating like the second hand of the clock, rapidly, and I could not even understand if that was it. I started walking towards my bike, but I was lost somewhere. I had already bid good bye to the staff members of the library, so I had no other reason to go in again. I started my bike and took off.

Next day, I was off to Pune, my plans for Bombay were postponed as I could not arrange for a job there. Moreover, the accommodation was not arranged as well. In Bombay, it's easy to get a job, lavish food and women but accommodation, VERY difficult. My main concern was accommodation.

So I changed my plans and thought of staying in Pune for a while. My family was happy to see me back especially my father. As I was away from him and there was no one to argue with him.

"How have you been, son?" he asked.

"I am good, dad," I said, and touched his feet. It had been six long months since I had met them. I hardly spoke to them. My sisters took the luggage from me, I was looking like a coolie on the railway station.

"How are you?" asked my mom and kissed me on my cheeks.

All the pain or sorrow which I had after departing from Saloni vanished for a moment seeing my family by my side.

"You get fresh, have a cup of tea and breakfast and take some rest," ordered Mom.

"Yes sure" I said and went ahead to get fresh. I came back into the living room where everyone was sitting. My dad switched on the television set for his favorite news show.

"So how was your work and all, brother?" asked Mili my younger sister.

"Oh, it was good. Had loads of fun," I replied munching on my favorite Mom-made food which I had missed for quite some time.

I had a weak voice though, I guess they could make out what was happening. Maybe they are my family and would understand me. Moreover, they knew of me liking a girl but no one knew the latest. I finished my breakfast in haste and

171

went into my room to take some rest. I had taken a night bus from Belgaum, which got me in to Pune in the morning. After a few hours of rest, I got up around noon. Mom was busy in the kitchen and my youngest sister was watching TV, her beloved show on astrology. I wonder who invented these new age Babas who come on TV with their scary looks and guide people like my sister about their future. I got fresh and came into the living room.

"Got enough rest?" she asked me.

Yawning, I replied "Yes."

"Looks like you didn't," she said immediately. "Anyways, how is your girlfriend?" she asked me.

"She is fine I guess, we are no more together."

"What? You guys were pretty fine with each other, I mean you both were happy being together, right?" She put the TV on mute, being astonished with my answer.

"I know, but things change," I replied.

"Hmmmm. So how is your plan for Bombay?" She changed the topic after putting the TV off mute.

"Let's see, I need to get a job, and right now I want to be with you all for some time," I said.

We continued talking for hours, dad and my younger sister came for lunch.

Dad went ahead and made me an offer to join his business again.

"Why don't you come to the office from tomorrow?" he asked.

"Tomorrow would be too early dad," I replied as if I just come off a Mars expedition.

"It would keep you busy," said my youngest sister, who had just heard my love story.

Finally, it was decided that I would join dad for few months in his business, which I didn't like, honestly. However, I continued my good charm and got some new clients for dad and grew his business. We were not together when it came for execution, but yes we handled it quite well.

Six months passed, we were in April, 2002. I was busy helping dad, but I wasn't happy. And my heart was somewhere else, I always thought of Saloni. I was not ready to accept that it's over. I always felt that she is going to come back. And my love for her grew day by day. I used to compare every girl I saw, or I met, with Saloni. I spoke about her to everyone who knew me. This thing made me dig deeper into her. I never tried calling her, and we were not at all in touch. One day an old friend of mine Joy called me and informed that he has got a job in a BPO.

"Hey Nikhil, guess what? I have got a job in WNS Bombay in a pilot process," he said.

"Hey, that's great news!"

Joy happened to be my college buddy, we both studied for three years together and he flunked for few years. Finally, he made it for the bachelor's degree.

Call centers had started coming into India, and it was a new boom for the Indian industry, a great package, good working condition and fun.

"Do you know they are offering me quite a nice package, why don't you try?" he suggested.

"Me?"

"Yes, you, you wanted to go to Bombay right? They have an accommodation for outstation employees as well."

That rang all the bells for me. I met him and took all the information about the job. His date of joining was three weeks later, on May 16th 2002. I went for the interview, and saw so many young people queuing up for the jobs. I went through a series of rounds, written test, GD, personal interview and finally, I got the job. I can't say I was lucky, but yes I had learnt many things during my tenure in previous company. So the date was set 16th May, 2002, me and my friend, we were going to Bombay.

1 BOMBAY

Our reporting time was 1430 hours on 16th May, so we took the morning train, Pragati Express which departed at 0750 hours from Pune station.

"Finally, you have made it," smiled Joy.

I smiled back at him taking my eyes away from the scenery outside. I had a window seat, and Joy was in the middle with one more man occupying the third seat. By the time we reached Lonavala, we both had consumed 2 cups of tea each, as we scanned through the papers.

"Joy, what have they offered you, you haven't told me yet," I inquired.

"Oh, yes. Here is the offer letter," he

said pulling out an envelope from one of his bags. I took a look, and saw that it was quite less than my offer.

"What is yours? Show me," he said.

I pulled my offer letter from my bag. It looked like 2 swords were out and ready to take on one other.

"Oh, wow, that's more than me!" he exclaimed.

"Just twenty four thousand," I said. "It's not a big deal. Maybe it was because of my experience."

"Yes, I know."

We kept on talking for 2 hours, looking at the beautiful view outside in Lonavala. We reached Dadar at 11 am. We took a cab, and headed towards our destination Malad, where our office was located.

"Where do you want to go sir?" asked the cab driver.

"Malad, Mindspace," said Joy as he kept his bag on the carrier over the roof.

I kept one of my bags in the boot and the other one by my side. Joy occupied the front seat, and I sat behind alone.

"It's too hot out here Nikhil," Joy said. He was one of the lavish guys who loved to live in style and spend. It looked to me as if he was going to return the very next day.

This whole trip expense was to be reimbursed, the train, cab and anything on the journey. So we did not compromise on anything even in hiring a cab instead of a local train to the office from Dadar. It took three hours from Pune to Dadar, but took another 75 minutes to reach Malad. Traveling in Bombay was a pain and is not too different today as well.

"Man what is this? To cross one signal we have to wait three times," said Joy.

I looked at him and just kept quiet in the face of his impatience.

"Bhaiyya, how long will it take to reach Malad?" he asked the driver.

"If the traffic ahead is like this, may be 30 minutes," replied the cab driver.

At that time, we were already 30 minutes old in the cab.

Poor guy, what would he do with the traffic here? Everyone wanted to come to Bombay. And it was the same with me and Joy. After honking, cutting through traffic and breaking a few traffic lights which the driver did on our request, we finally reached the office at 1230 hours.

"So here we are finally," said Joy.

I stepped out of the cab while Joy paid for the ride. I saw the name 'Intelnet' written on a tall glass building.

"Wow, this is awesome!" I said, still looking at the huge

premises. These were the first few words which I spoke after reaching Bombay. I had been a mute spectator while Joy had been doing all the talking. Meanwhile, we unloaded the luggage out of the cab. While we were walking with our luggage towards the lobby through the cafeteria, everyone looked at us. In fact, we had entered from the wrong side. We had to cross the cafeteria and then go to the lobby. The dining area was so huge that we were speechless and the way it was designed was fantabulous. The concept of call centers was really rocking, good package, great atmosphere and of course fun.

"This is gigantic man, what do you say Nikhil," asked Joy as he looked around 360 degrees taking an opportunity to glance at the ladies sitting there.

"No doubt," I replied with a smile.

We continued walking and reached the lobby. We informed the admin department that we had landed in the office.

"Hey guys, so you are here, haan?" said the admin guy Anthony with a funny smile on his face, which looked as if he has been designed to say this at this time, when someone enters.

We looked at each other and smiled at him.

"Damn it, of course we are here, on serious business, don't tell me you guys were joking with us with that offer letter and all," I wanted to say.

"Ok, we have the induction starting at 1430 hours. You can get fresh, and I will arrange for food coupons, you can have lunch," he said.

"And yes, once the induction is over you will be taken to your accommodation"

We followed him in the office, kept the luggage in one of the cabins. He handed over food coupons, which helped us to have our lunch. We went to the food counter and helped ourselves.

"Hey Joy, this place looks good man," I said.

He was busy chewing the butter chicken which the menu offered us for lunch. Once he was done pushing the chicken down his throat which was as huge as a Sintex water tank he said, "Hmm yes, besides the chicken the women here are hot."

We were surrounded by pretty faces which we were busy gazing at, while eating dessert.

"Absolutely," I said. I was not interested in them though, but they really were rocking.

We were in no hurry to finish the food as after four hours of journey, that is, three hours of train and more than an hour in the cab which was not an air conditioned one, it made us feel better to sit under the AC vent, eat a good four course meal and watch some sweet looking girls around. Joy was on cloud nine and me just beside him.

Finally, he got up and I followed suit. We passed some time outside in the premises until it was 2 pm. During the induction, we came to know that we were in 2 different batches for the training which would continue for 2 months. We were around 48, 24 in each batch. We both were not happy to be divided into 2 teams. But then there was a reason to smile, post induction, we were taken to the apartment.

1 ROOMMATE

We were put up in the office accommodation. It was a huge building leased by the company. While on our way when the car took a turn after the Malad Bridge, we were scared for a moment as we entered a slum, we could literally see some people selling roast meat right next to a garbage bin. Yikessss...

"Where the hell are we going?" said Joy.

I was looking out of the window, and even I was surprised to see such an approach.

"Where are we going?" I asked the admin guy Anthony, who was sitting on the front passenger seat.

"To your new house, it's just a bit

ahead," he replied.

Joy and I, we both exchanged looks. The place which we were passing by was a pathetic area. It was stinking like hell, we could smell it as we were popping out eagerly to see our new home from the open windows. After a breathless ride for a few minutes, we came out of that area and could see some beautiful buildings. It was the Raheja's in Malad east. The whole area was Raheja's. Our driver pulled over and entered an ok looking gate. It was kind of a steep upward slope.

"Wow, now we are talking," said Joy to Anthony.

We got down from the car with sheer excitement.

"This way," said Anthony, pointing towards the small entrance of C wing where he guided us.

We quietly followed him as we were anxiously waiting to see the final apartment after going through that hell.

We got into the lift which stopped on the second floor.

"After you," said Anthony after holding the lift shutter open for us. He was really kind to us.

"Hey thank you!" we both said at one go to Anthony for his sweet gesture of holding the lift open. To our surprise when Anthony opened the door of our flat, we were flattered.

"Wow, this is amazing," said Joy, and I just kept quiet for a moment as I was glancing around. As we both were looking around and checking the house, Anthony shouted from inside.

"Hey guys, come here,"

As we walked into the bedroom, he continued saying, this would be your room. Trust me that was a neat house and a nice bedroom.

"Who stays in the other bedroom?" I inquired.

"2 more guys would join you soon, no one yet," he replied.

We exchanged looks again, with our eyebrows going up, then we shrugged our shoulders. It was like saying who cares?

Alright guys, if you need any help feel free to call me, and yes, no women, and no loud parties.

"What?" said Joy as if he had been ordered a life sentence.

He looked back at us surprised. "No women, and no parties," he repeated.

We just kept quiet this time around, never even thought of asking him anything else. May be the same question "WHAT?!!" was lingering in Joy's mind, my mind was at ease.

Anthony left us with our new house. There was almost

everything in that flat, well-furnished kitchen, with refrigerator, microwave, gas connection.

The bedroom had a huge wardrobe and 2 single beds, with a huge sliding window. Joy was more interested to peep out into other houses instead of checking our home.

"Hey Joy, what are you doing?" I asked.

"Checking if there are any hot neighbours," he replied as he continued peeping out.

There was a nice drawing room, the only thing missing was the television set.

We both lay down on the beds. On our individual beds, I mean, don't think otherwise.

"Nikhil, this is a beautiful place man, let's celebrate," said Joy.

"Yes of course, this is a nice place. Let's celebrate!"

We both got up and started getting dressed.

"You know what, you should always know where the liquor shops and the medical shops are!" Joy shouted from the bathroom as he cleaned his sins and was getting ready for some fresh ones.

I understood the liquor shop, however, I was wondering why this alcoholic wants medical shop information.

"Medical shop, for what?" I inquired.

"Man if you don't want to invite trouble, go into the nearest medical shop and buy a packet of condoms," he said giving me a high five as he stepped out with a towel wrapped around him.

We both moved out. Our mission was to check around every store and lane in the vicinity. There were 2 back to back medical stores right under our building, Joy was happy to see them so close. Besides, there was an aunty managing one of the drug stores.

"Don't be surprised if the month's stock of condoms comes free," he said as he gestured at me to glance at the shop, where the aunty stood. He sure was a handsome guy and there was no doubt if that happens, one day I could find her too in my house, I realized.

After walking for around 500 meters, we found a liquor shop. We bought a Bacardi quarter and a KF mild chilled beer. Rum for the man and beer for me(n).

"Do you have a home delivery facility," asked Joy to the cashier in the wine shop.

"Above 150 rupees, sir," he replied.

Joy got in talks with that man and finally convinced him to arrange delivery for any amount. This guy was surely a great guy when it came to PR, which just became a history for me.

He took the store number, and we saw a cold storage right next to the wine shop. It was like cherry on the cake. We both were great fans of pork and almost any meat, we picked some Salami and Ham, for the time being. It sure was a celebration of our new job, new city and a new home. On our way back, I saw a huge Preity Zinta poster being sold on the road side, and I was a big fan of her, especially because she looked like Saloni.

"Take Salma Hayek instead," said Joy.

"You buy her," I replied.

"I don't believe in posters, when you have all the hot women, around," he said.

I bought Preity for pretty cheap, went home and put her on the wall next to my bed.

1 RESTART

It was an afternoon shift from 2 to 11 pm during the training and then fun as usual. In 2 weeks' time, we had our final 2 roommates. One was Shailendra Singh from Dehradun, and the other one was Clinton from Goa.

Shailendra was a somber, heavy duty guy around 5.9" and weighing 85 – 90 kgs. He brought a television set in the house which we badly needed, which we never thought would be used for BAD purposes going ahead. Clinton was a dark guy with a big thorn pierced in his left ear. It looked as if he had come straight from the jungles of Africa. He too was a man made for wine and women. Even he got something, guess what? One carton of beer, and a packet of Durex.

"You guys can please use this whenever needed," Clinton said as he unpacked the big packet of Durex.

I and Shailendra we were into these things but not completely, just a bit of beer sometimes, and yes, I was getting into women.

"Please keep it in a place accessible to all," said Joy.

We just needed a reason to celebrate and every small moment in our house was to be grand. Every other weekend, an office party was held at our apartment, it was not official yet official. So now, we had not only my team members coming in but Joy's, Shailendra's and Clinton's as well. It was a party house, security guards were bribed by all of us, whoever was hosting a party. Slowly, everything started looking good and yes, different as well.

"Hey Nikhil where are you lost?" asked Clinton one day during lunch.

I got myself back from wherever I was and answered him, "Nowhere, I am here with you guys."

They say women and alcohol are related, whenever you drink you are thrown out by your woman and whenever she dumps you, or you remember her, you drink. Saloni was in my mind whenever two pegs were down, and I was up in the sky on cloud ten where they say is a lost and found department.

"If you are with us, why is your glass still filled with beer when ours is shouting, FILL ME UP!" said Joy shouting out the latter part.

"Oh, yes. Take it easy man, please go ahead," I said.

"Look at Shailender, he is on his third peg," said Clinton.

Shailender happily raised his glass with a smile like Prem Chopra's, as if he was holding the Formula One trophy beating Schumacher in all the races.

We all raised our glasses and continued for some more time until we wound up.

Days passed by, our training got over, we did not understand where those two months flew. It was now our time to hit the floor.

"So friends, you would hit the floor and take your first call tomorrow," announced the trainer.

Everyone was excited and nervous as well. The shift I had to begin was from 9 pm to 6 am. It was called the graveyard shift. Joy was a bit lucky to have gotten the evening shift from 5 pm to 2 am. As they were all new concepts, we didn't realize the consequences.

"I am super excited!" said one of my colleagues the next day when we were ready to go live. I looked at him and smiled.

Calls started pouring in through the automated dialer like the uninvited guests at any wedding and there was no stopping.

"Hi this is Rachel, Am I speaking with Steve?" said one of my colleagues, who was sitting right next to me. Her name was Radhika, and she selected her pseudo name as Rachel.

I was planning to take up VIN PETROL, being inspired from Vin Diesel, but had to settle for Vin De Niro.

"Hi, is this Carmen Garcia?" I asked the person on the other end.

"Yes," she replied. "Who is this?"

"I am Vin De Niro."

She was a film buff and who can't be a Robert De Niro fan if you watch movies? She was not an exception. Guess what! She was my first client, and I struck gold. And that's how my other calls happened. Most of them were good, and some bad. Life being Vin De Niro was awesome.

Joy and me, we hardly met at home, awake. I started enjoying my days sleeping and having fun in the nights while working. I forgot the motive, for which I had come to Bombay. I was losing myself to the parties which happened to be so frequent. Women, whom no one can ignore in Bombay, I too surrendered to them. There was one thing, though which could not be erased out of my mind, Saloni.

Every person I met, I narrated my love story to them, even to the women I slept with. That's what kept me off from getting into a relationship.

All these things happened to me, and I spent one year doing all this. I did try to meet some of the film industry people, but in vain.

"I have a blurred year, behind," I told Joy one day, when we were sitting having a beer after a really long time.

"That's ok man, you are having fun at least," he replied.

I was in a serious mood finally. "I know, we have been having fun Joy. However, this is not what I came here for," I blew out.

He looked at me, kept his glass down and said, "So, what do you want me to do, or say what you want to do?"

I was quiet for a moment, as I knew I had lost the aggression or the thirst for music. "I believe it's never too late, let me start meeting more people," I replied. He picked up his glass and raised a toast, "Cheers, man." he said. We continued drinking until late and went to sleep. In a month, Joy left the company for good without serving his notice period and moved back to Pune. At the same time, Shailendra too left the company, he was having some family emergency. A new guy came, with new vibes in the house, his name was Sheen. Finally, some entertainment for my broken heart post Joy's departure and Shailender's as well.

"Hi, I am Sheen, Sheen John," he said.

"Hi, I am Bond, James Bond," I replied.

Clinton got up laughing from the sofa and introduced himself. "I am Clinton, welcome aboard."

Sheen shook hands with Clinton and looked at me, Clinton told him in his Yo style "He is Nikhil. He is a filmy man, expect all the filmy things." Clinton had this habit of bouncing and swinging as if something was itching down there.

Soon, Sheen and Clinton became buddies, while I went inside to take a shower. He was no exception to us, drinking, smoking, womanizing - everything in common. The only thing he had an add-on was his liking for porn films. Wow, that was something new to tag on.

I stepped out of my room and saw them talking. Sheen pulled out a mini DVD player out from one of his bags.

"This is what I have specially bought for my films, compatible and cheap," Sheen whispered.

He pulled out a packet of porn DVDs. "And this is the ammunition," he added.

"That's really an arsenal man" Clinton replied on seeing all that stuff, when Sheen handed them over to Clinton to run through.

I had to go to work and made my way out.

"Ok, guys have fun, bye."

"Hey, have fun working, man," Clinton said still busy watching the naked couples in different poses on the DVD covers.

Shailendra took his television set, but Sheen had his set accompanying him.

After talking, drinking and of course watching the lip-smacking videos all night long Sheen and Clinton became good friends. Sheen decided to share the room with Clinton, and I was spared. Sheen was not only a porn fan but a porn star as well. Every morning whenever I used to come home, he was seen lying on the sofa in the drawing room in different poses. I am sure he would have been fantasizing about some of those stars, just wonder if a fat man like him could star in those videos. But he was an entertainment in the house which filled in for Joy's place.

With all these new friends in this new city, I had forgotten my past, the person who was difficult to be forgotten. I used to remember her, whenever I used to come in contact with any girl. I kept myself off from getting into a relationship. I never understood what that was, but kept on thinking about her most of the time, reminiscing and cherishing my past.

One day at my Manager's birthday party I met someone. When I entered, I saw the drawing room lit with candles, and balloons spread across the floor, slow music in the background as the party was yet to be started. My Manager Amit and his fiancé Reema, were still decorating when I entered, while few of our colleagues helped them. They both knew me for all these years as we worked in the same office.

"Hey dude, thanks for coming," he wished me on my arrival throwing one more balloon on the floor.

"Wish you many happy returns of the day Amit" I said as I hugged him and handed over a metallic cigarette case which I got him as a gift.

"Hi Reema," I said as she was there right next to him and the other guys who continued decorating.

Amit was like Joy to me - a very good friend. He knew my love story completely and made all attempts to get me into a relationship whenever he got a chance.

"I am done sweetheart" he said to Reema as we parked ourselves on the black sofa. I looked around to the ambience which made the night look seductive.

Slowly, all the guests started pouring in, some from our office and a few from outside. Among all these people, there was one beautiful girl whom I was introduced to by Reema and Amit.

"Nikhil, meet Sia my best friend from college," said Reema. Sia was beautifully dressed, in a maroon, halter necked, knee length dress, which hugged her figure absolutely. She wore a mild perfume which complemented her attire and enhanced her looks.

"She is into PR (Public Relations), and he is a very good writer," added Amit.

"Oh, wow that's great," we both said for each other at one go.

There was a smile on my face and laughter on hers. Amit and Reema left us in quick succession to attend to the other guests, leaving us on our own.

"So, what all do you write Nikhil?" Sia began.

"Oh, me. I write on anything and everything that inspires me and makes me happy," I said.

"That's great, have you written commercially yet?" she asked as she sunk into the chair in one corner.

"No, I am trying my best," I said as I gulped my drink.

"Shall I get you a drink?" I asked her on seeing her empty handed.

She thought for a while "Ah, may be vodka with an orange juice"

Girls always preferred orange juice with vodka, to mislead people that they were having a plain orange juice.

"You should try vodka with apple juice instead," I said and

went to get one.

If you can make a woman happy with her drink and in the bed, then trust me, she is yours for life. After some time, the party began and there was a ballroom dancing organized by Amit, which was basically my plan. Everyone started dancing wherever they got a place to move as it was a huge room and people invited were around only 15. As Sia did not know many people around, she danced with Amit while I was gazing at the stars waiting in the balcony outside.

"Hey Nikhil, what are you doing here?" she asked as she came out and joined me.

"Looking at these beautiful stars flashing in the sky as if they are tweeting into our balcony," I said as I saw her coming and standing next to me leaning on the railing.

I still had the same drink which was almost over, and her drink was near to completion. We finished our drinks and went inside as Amit and Reema forced us on the dance floor. Reema joined me and Sia danced with Amit for some time, and then we exchanged partners.

"You dance really nicely," said Sia as she was still in my arms real close. For a flash, I was lost in Saloni but recovered in time as the song got over. Webecame good friends and met quite often either with Amit and Reema or on our own. A new ray of light came into my life, which was covered with darkness for a long time.

She knew about Saloni as every woman I met did. She was ok with it, and I knew that I was more than a friend for her but for me, she was only a friend. Life again started looking better and colorful with these friends.

However, my present had something else to present to me, my dad was to be operated in Pune.

"Nikhil, Dad is not keeping well. The doctors are suggesting an operation," my Mom told me on the phone one day.

"What? What happened to him?"

"His Hemoglobin level has gone down to 3.4, doctors say he has been losing blood."

Now that was a real surprise, HB level dropping down so badly was no joke.

"How come the level is 3.4? He has been fine, right? Then what happened suddenly?"

"You come here and we will talk," she said and ended the call while she sounded really scared.

I went to Pune on the day when my dad was to be operated on 8th Dec, 2005; he was operated with 14 stitches right in the middle of his stomach.

They said he was losing blood due to a small puncture in the intestine. Due to the doctor's negligence post operation, he got septicemia, and we lost him. He was in the ICU for 15 days, doctors charged us a bomb where we sold almost every gold ornament mom had. The doctors made money, and we built a grave for my dad. Doctors had no guilt whatsoever, and it was revealed that, the medicines which they prescribed were never given to him. Most of them made their way to the drug store downstairs through nursing assistants and doctors.

The sky came falling down on our family, and everything looked completely shattered. For me, it was the second impact in last three years. Once when Saloni left me and now when my dad passed away, this being the worst. My Mom was not able to come out of this, and my sisters were not ready to accept what happened. And I was cursing myself for not being here with him when he needed me.

"I am coming back to Pune," I told my Mom on the thirteenth day after his death.

She looked at me still in silence with her swollen eyes, but did not say a word.

I went to Bombay, and gave my resignation.

"I understand Nikhil and you are right, you have made the right decision," said my manager as I sat in his cabin.

"Thank you for understanding, Amit."

I served 2 months as my notice period and came to Pune. I never thought, "Change is the only thing constant in MY life." I mean so many changes. I remember that song which Gulzar wrote, "TUJHSE NAARAJ NAHI ZINDAGI, HAIRAAN HUN MAI." What all we do to stay alive and staying alive itself is not easy.

I started managing my father's business. I broke all contact with my friends just stayed at home with my family. I was in hibernation and became a complete recluse. My life had a downhill fall and was gradually going lower and lower.

1 LYRICS

THREE YEARS LATER (2008)

One thing that kept me going was my writing. I kept on writing whenever I was home, and that paid dividends. I wrote around 960 songs since the time I started writing (2001). I did shift base to Bombay as this time, I never wanted to take a chance. Bollywood or any industry, for that matter, gives you an opportunity only if you have been there and done it, or if you are the son of Mr. Bachchan or some Kapoors. I always wondered "If a person doesn't begin, how can he have something in his kitty?" or let me say everybody has to start from 0; nobody is born with experience right? Moreover, how many kids would the Bachchans and Kapoors raise?

With many fiascos of film songs being cancelled either due to production issues, direction issues, and my films getting shelved, I never got a start.

Sometimes it happened due to the actresses as well, who ran away with the director, taking away all the producer's money and leaving all their clothes behind.

"Great God, save this planet... Bollywood!" I used to say as I tried to find Him in the sky but always found smoke and Kingfisher or Jet Airways planes flying high, instead.

After a really long wait in the industry, my first song was released in the film "Daddy Cool," the song was "Nasha, Nasha" which made a ripple with women dancing in sparse clothes. There was no looking back, and I went ahead and did around 8 movies in just 5 months.

"Your songs are being hammered on the TV Nikhil, your name is popping up every other minute," said Sia, who was one of the few people I was in touch with.

"Hey, thanks a lot Sia, how are you?

"I am doing great, the industry is talking about you, congratulations!"

I used to meet her whenever I got time, and we were still good friends.

"You know what? I have to mail some songs, can I call you back?" I asked Sia.

"Why not, first things first, take care," she said and hung up.

I went through the songs which I had written for a new project and mailed them. As I was logging out Zainab sent me a message on my gmail.

"Hey, hw ya dng?"

Firstly, I did not understand what that was? I am not a net buff nor do I chat online. It was all Greek which looked like African to me.

"What?" I replied.

"I mean, how you doing?" she replied.

"Oh, I am fine; you tell me how you are?" My messages were full with no grammatical mistakes. Ten on ten marks scored.

"I m 5ne, u no wt, I pasd my exm and I ve gt a job 2."

I tried to weave all the words and connect them together for the meaning she wanted to convey. Trust me, it was like appearing for CET exams which I always avoided. It was after almost three years I was talking to her.

Whenever I made my trip to Belgaum during Ganapati, I made sure I met her until I lost my dad. She was a good person but the reason for me to connect with her was different. Every time the discussion revolved around Saloni and all I said was "I feel she is going to come back." For 4 years, I bugged her with the same talks. I am sure she was happy that we hadn't met for the last three years, or that we were not in touch.

We had a long conversation, oh let me say a tricky conversation about her work and my work. She told me that she had shifted back to Bombay, and she was working in Char Bangla area of Andheri. And the co-incidence was I was put up in the same area for the last six months. And her workplace was hardly 500 meters from my house, so we decided to meet.

I was waiting for her at a Yari Road coffee shop which was the best place to meet. You can buy a coffee and sit there for hours, In fact, most of the people just sit and don't even order anything, God have mercy on the outlet! She, as usual, came late.

"There you are, handsome!" she said as she saw me fiddling with my phone on one of the tables in the open.

"Ah, when are you going to be in time, lady?" I said as I glanced at my watch.

"Don't call me lady, I am a girl, Ok?" she said pointing her index finger at me in anger and thumping her bag on the table. She was the same, nothing had changed in her, they say everyone changes with time, but this girl did not, even after 6 years.

"Hey, that's cool. I am kidding and any ways you are late. Take a seat."

She made herself comfortable on the chair, and I could hardly see her as the bag, she kept on the table was too huge.

"What all do you carry in this bag? It's so huge, unlike you," I said as I picked the bag and kept it aside. When I lifted the bag it made some rattling noise.

"Be careful," she said as I banged it on the chair next to me.

"Whoooof, what all is stuffed in there?"

"Nothing to interest you, any ways how is everything at home and with you?" she asked me.

"Oh, going on well, they are happy that I have made it to song writing."

"Oh, wow, so you're still writing, haan?"

"Of course yes, and only writing now-a-days"

"Great, ya...even I passed out last year," she said as if she had cracked the world's biggest crossword puzzle. In fact, she should have been happy and there was a reason for it. She studied for six years with the course material for 4 years, great isn't it?

She gave me the surprise of my life that Saloni was back in

India. I was lost for some time listening to the conversation we had.

"Hey you know what? I saw Saloni on the Orkut Delhi singles community. I am wondering, why?"

"How come? She was getting married right?" I inquired. In fact, when I had met Zainab in the year 2006, Saloni was supposed to get married and shift her base to the US.

"Yes that's what I know, and that's what is bothering me," she replied. "Moreover, she is not responding to my emails, the last conversation we had was 2 years ago," she said. Saloni passed out of her college in 2005 and was planning to move to the US for her further studies. Moreover, Zainab had heard that she was getting married.

"What are you saying? Don't you have her home phone?"

"I did but I don't have it any more, guess I have misplaced it somewhere," she apologized

I was tense, so was she after seeing me like that. She finally said something.

"Hey, I got an idea," Good intentions right, a dumb person like her can also ideate, wow. She immediately stood up and got going.

"Hey, what happened? Where are you going?" I asked her thinking if this was her idea to escape the bill being shared between us.

"Will call you," she said and left.

I did not understand what she was up to. I paid the bill and went home. I did not sleep for too long that night as I had so many thoughts running through my head. Has she been married? Is she alright? And if she was married then why on the singles community? All these thoughts were running through my head like the local trains, after every fraction of a second.

Next day, early in the morning, I received a call from an unknown number.

"Hello,"

"Hi Nikhil," said someone on the other end. It was a girl's voice.

"Hi, who is this?" I asked.

"Guess who?" she said.

I was thinking for some time that the voice sounded familiar. Is it the same voice which I have been waiting to hear all these years? Is it the same person whom I have been thinking all the time about for seven long years?

"Saloni?" I whispered, in a faltering voice.

"Hey, how did you guess it right?" she asked.

I was quiet for a moment as if it was a dream, "How can I forget your sweet voice?" I said, still shaken.

She was way too happy, and I was overwhelmed to have her on the other side of the phone. We started talking, and she told me that she had shifted to Pune to be with her sister with many things having happened in her life.

"There are many things which I will tell you once we meet, but I am happy for you," she said.

"Thanks a lot Saloni, we will surely meet I am just caught up this week."

"No issues, may be next week or anytime when you have time, I am not going from here now," she said.

"Wow, that's great. I will connect with you. This is your number, right?"

"Yes, it's mine. Call me whenever you have time, and we shall meet," she said and we ended the call.

1 WISH

The day came when my dreams were to turn into reality, and my prayers were about to be answered. I was about to meet that person after seven years whom I always cherished and felt by my side. "Do I look good? Hope this T-shirt is ok, or shall I wear her favorite color?" I said to myself looking into the mirror while I got ready for the D-day. I would have never spent so much of time in front of the mirror as I did that day.

"Say hi to her," said my sister as I drove out of my parking lot.

"I will," I said as I made my way out in the car towards FC road, which was 10 kms away from where I stayed. I left few minutes early taking the Pune traffic into consideration. Pune's traffic has been growing like the Indian population.

"Hey, watch out, you stupid!" I said to a man who was driving in his old Maruti 800 right in the middle of the road despite me honking from behind.

On reaching the venue at 11, I saw someone identical to Saloni waiting outside the restaurant. As I parked my car and approached her, this girl had a smile on her face, the same which I left back years ago. Now I knew it was her, but she looked different. Much leaner or we can call it "size Zero." I had a bunch of daisies and a lotus stuffed in it which I managed to buy on my way.

"Hi Nikhil," she said with the smile expanding on her face and lifting her cheeks up making the day much brighter as I approached her.

"Hi Saloni, I hope I am not late" I asked as I went and stood in front of her while she continued her smile.

"No, not at all. In fact, I came in a bit early."

"Hey this is for you," I said as I handed over the bouquet.

"Hey, wow, that's awesome," she said, and we both avoided eye contact and looked ateverything other than each other. It was obvious, we were meeting after such a long time and that too with a bitter break off.

"Shall we go inside?" she said as her anxious face said she had so many things to share.

We went inside and found a place to sit in the backyard of Vaishali, the front portion was over packed as usual, it being a very famous joint.

"You haven't changed a bit Nikhil, you are absolutely the same," she said, looking at me again. She definitely had changed, was sounding much more mature than what she was before.

"But you have changed a lot, look at you, you've lost so much weight," I said as I faltered and sounded apprehensive.

"Oh that," she smiled "I have lost weight so that I can be fit. Besides, everyone feels I look better this way. What do you say?"

"I think you looked more beautiful then, and anyhow, you would always be the most beautiful person for me even at the age of 60."

Her eyes turned moist, meanwhile the waiter made an entry like the redeemer with 2 glasses of water, which he thumped on the table and pulled out a pen, stacked behind his right ear and held his tray underarm, taking out a note pad from his trousers to take down the order. He did not say a word, just stood there looking at us like a statue ready to write the history on the order sheet. We looked at each other and made our decision.

"One Onion Uttappa and a Club Sandwich," she said, with a cup of coffee for me and a fresh lime juice for her.

We placed our order and made him disappear for the next ten minutes.

"Any ways, congratulations to you on making your dream come true," she said.

"Hey, thanks a lot. Life is shaping up and looking better now," I said as I tried to smile.

"That's great, I am happy for you. I am so sorry, I made a wrong decision leaving you," she said as tears rolled down her eyes. I couldn't see her crying and didn't do anything any ways, other than being a worried spectator. The waiter came with our order, which made her simmer down a bit, he placed it on the table.

"Are you alright?" I asked getting my elbows down on the table and resting my chin over my folded knuckles as she wiped her tears with the tissues kept in front. The waiter stood there watching her as if the tissues were worth a million, or maybe he felt really bad that she was crying and thought I was the reason. Sitting in front of her, I felt I will be bashed by women activists anytime, for making a girl cry and of course by the waiter as well. I turned around to see, if there are any of those women around. Nowadays, all the politicians or any social worker are more concerned with publicityand mileage. It hardly makes any difference to them if anyone cries or smiles as long as they are in the spotlight.

"Hey, please do not cry, you didn't do anything wrong. It was my mistake, if I wouldn't have hurt you and given you a chance to leave me, you would not have been far." I tried to soothe her down.

"No Nikhil," she said controlling her tears "It wasn't you, it was me who left you."

She finally threw a big grenade on me, which would kill me for 100 years every minute. She told me that she got married 2 years ago, and her relationship didn't work out as expected. She was on the verge of getting divorced.

"What?" was my reaction as I sat there staring at her, and few more tears made their way out from her eyes. Why do bad things happen to good people? I mean, I agree that she left me but that wasn't wrong, I deserved it. She moved to USA for one year and had been here with her sister for a year now, post her marriage.

"You know what? I always felt you are going to come back to me one day. My friends, very close friends laughed at me when I shared it with them. I really don't know what it was, but I knew you would be here with me one day," I said as the emotional bomb in my heart exploded and sent out a few drops of tears to my eyes too.

"I am back now," she said with a smile, and excitement

immediately showing on her face, mopping her tears off with another tissue. She looked the same old sweet girl, but she controlled herself in no time. "I mean I am back in India."

"I know you have come, but I never thought of you returning this way. I mean I always prayed for you, all my wishes were in your direction and they all meant happiness for you wherever you are. I never thought I would see you like this," I said as my elbows my arms got sore, and I had to lean back.

We spoke for another hour where she told me the whole story and the reason for her divorce. This guy used to beat her under the influence of alcohol, and had various affairs outside. Our discussion went on for quite some time, but then she had to go somewhere, and I had to leave to Mumbai, so we got going at one thirty.

"Come, I will drive you back home," I said offering her a drive once we stepped out of the restaurant.

"No, no, I will take an auto," she said peeping into my eyes and hugging me tight. "Bye," she said and left. My eyes were moist too but still, being a man, I controlled it, could not see her like this.

I thought those years which went in pain, were a bad dream, and I was still in 2001. However, the fact remained that I couldn't forget her miserable face. I went to Bombay and for

4 days I did not answer anyone's phone calls other than my family members. Sia called me for almost 27 times in those days.

"Hi there, how are you?" I said as I called Saloni after thinking for a really long time.

"Hey, I am fine. Nice to hear from you" she said, delighted with my call.

"Where are you? In Pune, or Mumbai?"

I had forgotten that Bombay was no more called by the old name but Mumbai, and it really sounded good when she said it.

"I am in Mumm..Mumbai, hoping to visit Pune next weekend," I said trying to get the city's name correct, as she did.

Meanwhile, there was a call waiting and that was none other than Sia.

Wow, now this is what we call a co-incidence. I was in a bad situation and definitely in trouble this time around.

"Hey, I have an important incoming call, we shall talk later," I said to Saloni and hung up on her and dialed Sia. I knew that now I can't avoid Sia.

"Hey where are you? What's up with you? I have been trying to get in touch with you for the past few days, what's happening?" She fired all the questions at one go when I called back. I could understand she was pissed.

"Hi Sia, I am sorry… I…" she abruptly cut me short…

"I was so worried about you until I called your Mom today, that's when I came to know you are fine."

"That's what I am saying, I…." Again, she jumped in and cut me by half, trust me, there are some times when women act weird, and you can't do anything at all other than keeping quiet.

"Please don't do anything like this again," she said in an angry voice running out of breath, exactly as a car reacts when running out of fuel. "And yes, I want to meet you," she ordered, adding, "Now," after a slight pause.

Wow, what a nice time to be stuck like this. She was my friend but yes this was the first time she behaved like she owned me and that too for free.

"Ok, where do you want to meet?" I asked, to pacify her. Soon she cooled down and told me the place and time where I would be further grilled.

I met her in time to avoid things getting out of hand. After entering the coffee shop I looked for her, there she was sitting in one corner table facing inside.

"Hi, Sia," I said and placed myself onto the sofa sliding inside.

She didn't say a word and was looking at the menu in her hand, so I asked the steward to get a glass of water, Cappuccino for myself and her favorite Café latte for the Madam.

"No, I will drink a cold coffee instead," she said to which the waiter made a note. However, she still didn't say a word to me.

"Hey, I am sorry I did not answer your call. In fact, I was caught up with something really important," I said as she shifted her eye barrel from the menu to my face. She looked ready to launch a grenade and threw the menu on the table.

"And what was that important thing?" Bulls eye, she asked, hitting my MiG20 to collapse on the ground when I thought I was flying high to escape that bad sector of questioning.

"The thing is…." my phone rang and interrupted me. "A narrow escape," I thought to myself breathing a sigh of relief. I pulled the phone from my pocket and to my surprise, it was Saloni. "Oh!" was my reaction while my eye balls popped out as if hanging there, I looked up at Sia and then at the screen again. Oops second aircraft is down.

"Not an important call," I said as I put the phone on silent putting it back from where I pulled it.

"You were saying something," she said trying to get that important thing. Girls are like a broken record which keeps on playing in the loop mode.

"Oh, ya. The thing is…ahh, there is this song which I was supposed to finish by tomorrow, and it's for a really big film," I said wavering and breaking while I did the talking.

"But that doesn't mean you can't take out a minute to call back for someone who has been calling for so long!"

"I know I could have, but sorry I didn't." A woman can be a pain in the ass if she gets into interrogation and especially when she is in love with you, which you are not aware of.

Somehow I managed to get rid of her attempt, and she was convinced.

"You know I don't hide anything from you, right?" I said and held her hand in mine. "You are the only person who is so close to me and such a sweet friend," I added. Finally, that brought a smile on her face. At any point of time if you are stuck in a conversation with a girl and have no way out just say these words and hold her hand.

We sat there for more than three hours, talking nothing great and no great business to the coffee shop as well. We just had a single drink each which we kept on sipping until the cups touched rock bottom and the bill came to only 132 rupees. That's the best thing a coffee shop offers you "TIME." Buy a coffee sit there sipping it up and make sure you don't let it get over.

So in no time i.e., in a few days my life was just like a basketball juggled from one hand of Saloni to the other of Sia and

God definitely being like Michael Jordan.

"What am I doing?" I said to myself when I realized lying had become a part of my day to day life. I had no answer, but I knew I had to stop it somewhere as I was going nowhere.

"Hi Sia, how are you?" I said as I made up my mind to tell her the truth.

"I am fine and how are you Mr. Writer?" she said.

"I am doing good. I wanted to meet you"

"Wow, for a change that sounds great, lets catch up, lets sayyyyy....hmmmm around 9?" she said, with loads of visualization, I guess.

"Any chance of meeting, a bit early say around eightish?" I asked timidly.

"No yaa, I would love to, but then I have this meeting happening in town for the movie which I told you has been getting delayed for months. I am sick of this film as I have lost three months of my time in it. However, yes 9 is sure," she said.

We agreed to it and decided to meet at our favorite coffee shop.

I went there exactly at 9 and tried to locate her but in vain as she had not come in. So I waited until it was 9.30, when I called her up which she did not answer. She sent me a text

"Just left, in the cab with The Director, see u soon, sorry."

When she came it was 1015, and I was waiting there like an idiot until then.

This was the first time when I had 2 cups of coffee already in an hour's time. The waiter was looking at me surprised.

"Hey Nikhil I am soooo sorry for making you wait. But this film ya, I am fed up of it!"

She started immediately after entering. "I was stuck there in this promotion campaign, of this film and I have not been able to take any project since I took this in hand. I just want to get over it."

"I can understand," I said.

She called the waiter and asked him for a Cappuccino and Café Latté.

"Tell me, how was your day?" she asked settling down placing her bag and belongings on the sofa next to her.

"It was kind of ok" I said as I cried off it being good.

"Why? What happened to you? Hope everything's alright?" she said coming forward and holding my hand.

Now this gesture and concern for me were too much, and it was clear that she was definitely not taking me as a friend.

"In fact,, I wanted to meet you as there is something really important, I wanted to talk to you."

"Yes, why not, tell me."

"Saloni is back in India, and I met her last week in Pune," I said and the waiter came with the coffee and asked us for whom Cappuccino was?

"What?" she said leaving my hand on the table and leaning backward, the waiter got scared, I believe he felt that 'What!' was for him, for the question he asked, but that dumb person would have guessed the cappuccino beingmine, as I already had finished 2 and we were regular customers. I guess they pay less attention to the people who spend less in their outlet.

"Cappuccino is mine and Latte for the madam" I said to him.

"What are you saying? Saloni is back? And what is she doing in Pune?" she said.

"Loads of things ya, she is with her sister who lives in Pune."

"And what did she say to you?" she said getting more curious and putting me in big trouble instead of helping me out, which I thought she could.

"She didn't say much, she said she is back and would be here in Pune now."

That changed everything, Sia almost started crying. This was difficult for me handling both the ladies crying, and I had to make a choice now.

"So what are you thinking now?" she asked perplexed "Anyways, you always felt she is coming back, right?"

"Yes I did but I don't know what to do now, that is why I wanted to share it with you."

"What? I am not your friend ok, that you come and tell me your love story. I don't know if you understand, but I love you!"

As soon as she said that, she grabbed her belongings and left.

"Hey, Sia, what happened?"

She didn't bother to answer me, and continued walking towards the door, and I followed her. Getting embarrassed and making girls cry, had become a favorite pastime for me.

"Hey come on, what happened? Will you stop and talk at least?" I said holding her wrist as she made an exit from the coffee shop.

She turned around looking at me with her eyes squeezing out liters' of water.

"We have been together for more than three years now, you know that you are more than a friend to me, don't say you don't know that I love you."

I felt as if my heartbeat stopped, everything around me

vanished, and it was only me and her there. "I…." I said trying to answer her but couldn't say other than "I." In fact, I never loved her, and she knew it, it was a deal of friendship. But I guess that's how the love bug gets onto you and kisses your senses good bye. Like Shahrukh said in Kuch Kuch Hota Hai "Dosti hi Pyaar hai" (Friendship is Love). I didn't try to stop her but saw her going.

That night as I went back home and lay on my bed, a series of flashback was seen all over my room, starting from the days of Saloni till date. I felt, as if there is a projector connected somewhere, which had all my walls glowing with memories good and bad. I tried to connect in bits and pieces to arrange them together, in order to shape up my messed up life. I knew I had lost a major chunk of my life without someone's love and this time, I had to make a decision so that, my future holds my hand, and gives me that person whom I can love and grow old with.

I L♥VE

With night long thinking and puffy eyes in the morning, I came to a conclusion and dialed a number.

"Hi Saloni, how are you?" I said as she answered the phone.

"Hey, I am good and you?"

"I am doing good thank you. I just wanted to know, if we can meet tomorrow," I asked her straight with a great confidence.

"Tomorrow!!!!! Is evening fine with you?" she asked.

"Yah, it's absolutely fine."

I don't know what she thought, but I was excited to meet her. I was feeling like a bird, flying high under the red sky painted with love. I missed this wonderful feeling in the last seven years. "Now that's a million-dollar smile," I said posing before the mirror, with a broad hearty smile on my face. There was no news of Sia, and even I did not try to take the initiative to call her up as I thought first things first.

The next day, I went to Pune and as discussed met Saloni at FC road, and drove her down to Ambrosia near NDA.

"Hey, nice T-shirt," she said as she got into the car and sat on the passenger seat. That was the first time she was sitting in my car. You won't believe I had kept the front passenger seat vacant for three years and did not have any girl (friend) sit on it as I always wanted Saloni to sit there.

"Thank you, you look stunning as usual," I said as I handed her a bouquet of red roses and not her favorite flower for a change. I made our way pass through the traffic on the university road towards Ambrosia. I wanted a nice place to sit and talk to her besides this restaurant has a great view, and is located on a hill top.

"Where are we heading?" she inquired as we turned left from the University circle.

"Surprise..."

She started looking around, as if this was the first time she visited this part of the town. We talked about our families, health, work everything until we reached the destination. We parked our car and walked up the hill towards the restaurant.

"This is a beautiful place, wow!" she said spreading her arms and looking at the city looking so pretty, when we reached the restaurant.

"Yes, this is a beautiful place and that's why I wanted you to come here."

We entered the restaurant it was 6.30 pm, and took a window side table the lights started glowing in the whole city slowly, which made the evening much better.

"Saloni, I hope you know how important you have been to me," I started as she paid attention to what I was saying once we sat on the table. "I still remember the day, for the first time, on that night ride that we went on. Every little thing is so clear to me, that I feel as if it happened just yesterday."

I could see the tears in her eyes as she knew she was the one for me, but it wasn't the same case with her. I mean, I don't know how many men she dated, but I still loved her.

"I know Nikhil" she said letting her head down.

"I don't know how to say this, but…" she interrupted me…..

"What is there to say?"

"Saloni as I said, all these years I have been waiting for you, and I knew one day you will come to me. And the reason why I loved you all the while you were gone is because I

227

cherished your memories and kept myself away from girls. I kept off from getting into any relationships."

"Hey, see jugnu," she said pointing out the window trying to change the topic. May be she was a bit nervous.

"Yeah," I said trying to locate the fly, and panned my eyes back to her.

"Hmmm, so where was I? Yes, I kept off from getting into any kind of relationship with women other than friendship. But, that did not help, I couldn't stop them having feelings for me."

"What?" she said

"In fact there is someone who loves me, someone who has been there with me for 3 years as a friend."

She had no idea where I was heading as she kept her eyes glued on me with a mild smile on her face. I know she had nothing to say, but I am sure she had that courage to hear what I had on my mind. I didn't blame her for whatever happened with both of us but yes, our decisions are responsible for our present and our future. I had made a decision, and I knew I couldn't change the past of Saloni but I definitely can't ruin someone's future.

"Saloni, firstly, I want you to promise me, that no matter what I say we will still be friends forever."

"Yes…of course" she said with a nervous expression on her face blended with a forced smile.

"There is a girl called Sia, who loves me, it's purely unconditional, I was unaware of it until yesterday. I always believed that I loved you, till date but I was wrong, I am incomplete without her."

She kept on nodding to whatever I said. "Whatever happened in your life is really bad, but it has happened and the damage is done. It's irreversible but if I break her heart, there would be one more person in the circle who would stop believing in love, and I would not want to do that. I hope you understand me."

"You are correct, you are absolutely right," she said clearing her throat wiping the drop of a tear surfacing in her right eye and leaning forward. "I don't believe in love now."

"You are wrong," I said, "that's what I did all these years and kept myself off from this beautiful feeling. I had somebody really special real close but my heart never felt the warmth of it. You know why? Because I was lost in the past, I was lost in something, which was not there and, which would have never been there with me. All I request you today is to live life in the present, don't sulk in the feeling of what happened yesterday, and what would have happened if you would have acted in a certain manner. Whatever has happened has already happened you cannot change it. However, you can change your present and future by living for today, believing in love." I finished a long speech with Saloni listening to me very carefully. She is really beautiful and sweet, but sometimes it's not only what you are that counts but what you happen to be at the right time and at the right place. I didn't let the discussion kill the evening, and we had some great conversation, with some mouth-watering food and left. That day we promised we would be friends forever unconditionally.

"God forgive me if I have hurt someone, I just wanted to keep someone happy and that's why I took this step," I said to myself taking a deep breath as I reached home after dropping Saloni to her place. That wasn't all - I had another task to be completed, and that was calling up my love….

Most of the times we run around looking for love, trying to find love, but these thing find you, and you have to be ready for it as it happens to be right next to you.

I went to Mumbai next day and proposed to Sia, which she couldn't believe.

On 14th February 2010 we got Married and till date we are best friends and best couple. Does every love story end with a zero? I don't think so...